Convers German Dialogues

50 GERMAN CONVERSATIONS TO EASILY IMPROVE YOUR VOCABULARY & BECOME FLUENT FASTER

CONVERSATIONAL GERMAN DUAL LANGUAGE BOOKS VOL. 1

TOURI

https://touri.co/

ISBN: 978-1-953149-20-6

CONTENTS

WANT THE AUDIOBOOK FOR FREE?

We have a **limited** amount of **free** promotional codes for this audiobook.

Here's how it works:

1. **Visit the link below** to see the listing on AudiobookRocket
2. Request a free promo code from us
3. In **30 days** leave an honest, unbiased review on the audiobook.
4. Confirm & notify us on AudiobookRocket that you left a review.
5. Request and enjoy additional audiobooks from other publishers on the site.

https://audiobookrocket.com/audiobooks/17

IF YOU ENJOY THE FREE AUDIOBOOK,

PLEASE HELP US OUT AND **LEAVE A REVIEW**

RESOURCES

TOURI.CO

Some of the best ways to become fluent in a new language is through repetition, memorization and conversation. If you'd like to practice your newly learned vocabulary, Touri offers live fun and immersive 1-on-1 online language lessons with native instructors at nearly anytime of the day. For more information go to Touri.co now.

FACEBOOK GROUP
Learn Spanish - Touri Language Learning

Learn French - Touri Language Learning

YOUTUBE
Touri Language Learning Channel

ANDROID APP
Learn Spanish App for Beginners

BOOKS

SPANISH

Conversational Spanish Dialogues: 50 Spanish Conversations and Short Stories

Spanish Short Stories (Volume 1): 10 Exciting Short Stories to Easily Learn Spanish & Improve Your Vocabulary

Spanish Short Stories (Volume 2): 10 Exciting Short Stories to Easily Learn Spanish & Improve Your Vocabulary

Intermediate Spanish Short Stories (Volume 1): 10 Amazing Short Tales to Learn Spanish & Quickly Grow Your Vocabulary the Fun Way!

Intermediate Spanish Short Stories (Volume 2): 10 Amazing Short Tales to Learn Spanish & Quickly Grow Your Vocabulary the Fun Way!

100 Days of Real World Spanish: Useful Words & Phrases for All Levels to Help You Become Fluent Faster

100 Day Medical Spanish Challenge: Daily List of Relevant Medical Spanish Words & Phrases to Help You Become Fluent

FRENCH

Conversational French Dialogues: 50 French Conversations and Short Stories

French Short Stories for Beginners (Volume 1): 10 Exciting Short Stories to Easily Learn French & Improve Your Vocabulary

French Short Stories for Beginners (Volume 2): 10 Exciting Short Stories to Easily Learn French & Improve Your Vocabulary

ITALIAN

Conversational Italian Dialogues: 50 Italian Conversations and Short Stories

PORTUGUESE

Conversational Portuguese Dialogues: 50 Portuguese Conversations and Short Stories

WANT THE NEXT GERMAN BOOK FOR FREE?

https://touri.co/premium-access-german-dialogues/

INTRODUCTION

So you're ready to take the plunge and learn German? What an excellent choice you have made to expand your horizons and open more doors of opportunities in your life.

If this is your first time or a continuation in your German learning journey, we want you to know that we're proud of you.

Did you know German is the third most commonly taught language worldwide? In fact, it is the 11th most-spoken language, with about 90 million native speakers. In Europe, however, it's the number one most common mother tongue, beating out Spanish, French, Italian, and even English. Roughly 16% of the European population speaks German as a first language.

Germany is famous for its world-renowned scholars and musicians. Albert Einstein revolutionized our understanding of science, Sigmund Freud transformed the study of psychology, and Johann Sebastian Bach changed the way we think about music. And though these Germans are household names in the English-speaking world, we tend to not know quite so much about the language that they spoke. For example, did you know that German nouns have three genders, or that the first printed book was written in German?

As you may know, learning a new language has a multitude of benefits that expand far beyond simply navigating through a conversation with a native speaker. The ability to communicate in a foreign language will allow you to truly immerse yourself in different cultures, create even more memorable travel experiences and become even more marketable for advancements in career opportunities.

It is human nature to naturally progress and learn from the day we are born. Since birth we have been shaping our preferences based on our previous experiences. These experiences have provided you important feedback about your likes, dislikes, what has made you better or worse and allowed you to learn from these lessons.

The same approach should be taken to learn a new language.

Our goal with this book is to provide engaging and fun learning material that is relevant and useful in the real German-speaking world. Some students are provided with difficult or boring language materials that cause the learner to become overwhelmed and give up shortly after.

Building a strong foundation of vocabulary is critical to your improvement and reaching fluency. We *guarantee* you that this book is packed with vocabulary and phrases that you can start using today.

WHAT THIS BOOK IS ABOUT & HOW IT WORKS

A sure-fire way to exponentially decrease your time to German fluency is to role play with key words and phrases that naturally occur in actual scenarios you experience on a daily basis.

This book has 50 examples of conversations, written in both German and English so you never feel lost in translation, and will ensure you boost your conversational skills quickly.

You will find each chapter different from the last as two or more characters interact in real life scenarios. You will soon learn how to ask for directions, send a package at the post office, call for help, introduce yourself and even order at a restaurant.

Sometimes a direct translation does not make sense to and from each language. Therefore, we recommend that you read each story in both languages to ensure understanding what is taking place.

TIPS FOR SUCCESS

No doubt you can pick up this book at anytime to reference a situation that you may be in. However, in order to get the most out of this book, there is an effective approach to yield the best results.

1. **Role-play**: Learning takes place when activities are engaging and memorable. Role-play is any speaking activity when you either put yourself into someone else's shoes, or when put yourself into an imaginary situation and act it out.

2. **Look up vocab**: At some points there may be a word or phrase that you don't understand and that's completely fine. As we mentioned before, some of the translations are not word-for-word in order for the conversations to remain realistic in each language. Therefore, we recommend that you look up anything that is not fully clear to you.

3. **Create your own conversations**: After going through all of the stories we invite you to create your own by modifying what you already read. Perhaps you order additional items while at a restaurant or maybe you have an entirely different conversation over the phone. Let your imagination run wild.

4. **Seek out more dialogues**: Don't let your learning stop here. We encourage you to practice in as many ways as possible. Referencing your newly learned phrases and vocabulary, you can test your comprehension with German movies and television shows. Practice, practice, practice will give you the boost to fluency.

Focus on building your foundation of words and phrases commonly used in the real world and we promise your results will be staggering! Now, go out into the world, speak with confidence and in no time native speakers will be amazed by your German speaking skills.

Good luck!

Basic Survival Phrases

Greetings

1. *Hallo* – Hello
   (Ha-low)

2. *Hallo, wie geht's?* – Hello, how are you?
   (ha-low, vee gits?)

3. *Guten Morgen* – Good morning
   (goot'n maw-g'n)

4. *Guten Tag* – Good afternoon
   (goot'n tahg)

5. *Guten Abend* – Good evening
   (goot'n ab'nd)

6. *Gute Nacht* – Good night
   (goot-eh na-kht)

7. *Vielen Dank* – Thank you very much
   (vee-lehn dahnk)

8. *Ich danke Ihnen auch* – Thank you, too [replying to "thank you" from someone else]
   (ikh dahn-keh ih-nen auk)

9. *Tschüss, bis zum nächsten Mal* – Goodbye, see you next time
   (choos, biss zoom nah-schten mahl)

10. *Mein Name ist...* – My name is _
    (Mine nah-meh ist ...)

11. *Ich bin Amerikaner, Kanadier, Engländer (male)* – I'm
American/Canadian/English
(ikh bin Ameri-kAh-ner, Kan-Ah-dee-he, Eng-lan-der)

12. *Woher kommen Sie?* – Where are you from?
(voh-hare koh-men see?)

13. *Freut mich* – Nice to meet you
(froyt mikh)

14. *Sprechen Sie Englisch?* – Do you speak English?
(spre-kehn zee eng-lisch?)

15. *Es tut mir leid* – I'm sorry
(Es toot meer layd)

16. *Ich weiß nicht* – I don't know
(Ikh vies nikht)

17. *In Ordnung* – All right
(en ord-noong)

18. *Macht nichts* – Never mind
(makht nikhts)

19. *Was bedeutet das?* – What does that mean?
(Vas beh-do-tet das?)

RESTAURANT

1. *Einen Tisch fuer eine Person bitte* – **A table for one please**
   (ey-ndn tish fuhr eyn-a per-zown bi-tuh)

   Einen Tisch fuer zwei Personen bitte – **A table for two please**
   (ey-ndn tish fuhr tz-vay per-zown-en bi-tuh)

2. *Haben Sie schon auf?* – **Are you open yet?**
   (ha-ben zee schun on?)

3. *Können wir (auf einen Tisch) warten?* – **Can we wait (for a table)?**
   (koh-nen veer on eyn-en tish var-ten?)

4. *Was ist das?* – **What's this?**
   (vas ist dahs)

5. *Können wir dort sitzen?* – **Can we sit over there?**
   (koh-nen veer dohrt sit-sen)

6. *Entschuldigung!* - **[Calling a waiter]**
   (Ent-shul-dee-gung!)

7. *Kann ich bitte die Speisekarte haben?* – **Can I have the menu, please?**
   (kan ikh bi-tuh dee spiis-uh-kar-tuh ha-ben?)

8. *Was empfehlen Sie?* – **What do you recommend?**
   (vas em-fee-len zee?)

9. *Was ist das beliebteste Gericht?* – **What's your most popular dish?**
   (Vas ist das be-lee-eb-test ger-eekht?)

10. *Die Rechnung, bitte* – **The cheque, please**
    (dee rekh-nung, bi-tuh)

TRANSPORTATION

1. *Ich möchte nach ____ – I want to go to _*
   (Ikh muhkh-tuh nakh ____)

2. *Wann fährt der nächste Zug / Bus nach __?* - **What time is the next train/bus to _ ?**
   (Vann fehrt der naykh-stuh tzoog/bus nakh ____?)

3. *Was kostet das?* – **How much is it?**
   (vas kos-tet das?)

4. *Einmal / zweimal (nach ____), bitte* – **1 ticket / 2 tickets (to ____), please**
   (eyn-mal / tz-vay-mal nakh, bi-tuh)

5. *Wie lange dauert das?* – **How long does it take?**
   (vee lang-uh dau-ert das?)

6. *Wohin muss ich jetzt gehen?* – **Where should I go now?**
   (vo-hin muss ikh yetz gay'n?)

7. *Wann fährt er ab?* – **When does it leave?**
   (van fehrt er ab?)

8. *Wie spät ist es (jetzt)?* – **What time is it (now)?**
   (vee spayt ist es yetz?)

9. *Hält der Zug / Bus in _?* – **Does this train/bus stop in ____?**
   (haylt der zoog / bus in ____?)

10. *Entschuldigen Sie, ist dies ____?* – **Excuse me, is this _?**
    [Helpful when you're on the bus/train and aren't sure when to get off]
    (Ehnt-school-dign zee, ist dees ____ ?)

NUMBERS

1. ***eins*** – one
   (ainz)

2. ***zwei*** – two
   (Tz-vay)

3. ***drei*** – three
   (DRR-ay)

4. ***vier*** – four
   (feer)

5. ***fünf*** – five
   (fuhnf)

6. ***sechs*** – six
   (zex)

7. ***sieben*** – seven
   (zee-behn)

8. ***acht*** – eight
   (ahkt)

9. ***neun*** – nine
   (noyn)

10. ***zehn*** – ten
    (tzen)

11. ***elf*** – eleven
    (elf)

12. zwölf – twelve
(zvehlf)

13. dreizehn – thirteen
(drr-ay-tzen)

14. vierzehn – fourteen
(veer-tzen)

15. fünfzehn – fifteen
(fuhnf-tzen)

16. sechzehn – sixteen
(zekh-tzen)

17. siebzehn – seventeen
(zeeb-tzen)

18. achtzehn – eighteen
(akht-tzen)

19. neunzehn – nineteen
(noyn-tzen)

20. zwanzig – twenty
(tzan-tzig)

21. einundzwanzig – twenty-one
(eyn-and-Tzan-tzig)

22. dreißig – thirty
(drr-ays-ig)

23. vierzig – forty
(veer-tzig)

24. fünfzig – fifty
(fuhnf-tzig)

25. sechzig – sixty
(zekh-tzig)

26. siebzig – seventy
(zeeb-tzig)

27. achtzig – eighty
(eight-tzig)

28. neunzig – ninety
(noyn-tzig)

29. hundert – one hundred
(huhn-durt)

30. tausend – one thousand
(tau-send)

THIS PAGE IS LEFT BLANK INTENTIONALLY

1. FORMELLE BEGRÜSSUNG – FORMAL GREETING

Hans: Guten Morgen Professor Justus, wie geht es Ihnen?

Professor Justus: Guten Morgen Hans. Mir geht es gut und Ihnen?

Hans: Mir geht es gut, danke. Das ist meine Freundin Klarissa. Sie denkt über die Anmeldung an dieser Universität nach. Sie hat einige Fragen. Macht es Ihnen etwas aus uns über den Ablauf zu erzählen?

Professor Justus: Hallo Klarissa! Es freut mich Sie kennenzulernen. Es wäre mir ein Vergnügen mit Ihnen zu sprechen. Kommen Sie bitte nächste Woche in meinem Büro vorbei.

Klarissa: Es freut mich Sie kennenzulernen Professor. Vielen Dank für Ihre Hilfe.

Professor Justus: Gerne. Hoffentlich kann ich Ihnen alle Fragen beantworten!

FORMAL GREETING

Hans: Good morning, Professor Justus, how are you doing?

Professor Justus: Good morning, Hans. I am doing well. And you?

Hans: I'm well, thank you. This is my friend Klarissa. She is thinking about applying to this university. She has a few questions. Would you mind telling us about the process, please?

Professor Justus: Hello, Klarissa! It's a pleasure to meet you. I'm more than happy to speak with you. Please stop by my office next week.

Klarissa: It's a pleasure to meet you, professor. Thank you so much for helping us.

Professor Justus: Of course. Hopefully, I will be able to answer your questions!

2. Informelle Begrüssung – Informal Greeting

Gottfried: Wer ist die große Frau neben Barbara?

Karl: Das ist ihre Freundin Marie. Hast du sie nicht auf Stefan´s Party getroffen?

Gottfried: Nein, ich war nicht auf Stefan´s Party.

Karl: Oh! Dann stelle ich sie dir jetzt vor. Marie, das ist mein Freund Gottfried.

Marie: Hi Gottfried. Schön dich kennenzulernen.

Gottfried: Ja finde ich auch. Möchtest du was trinken?

Marie: Ja, lass uns was trinken.

INFORMAL GREETING

Gottfried: Who's the tall woman next to Barbara?

Karl: That's her friend Marie. Didn't you meet her at Stefan's party?

Gottfried: No, I wasn't at Stefan's party.

Karl: Oh! Then let me introduce you to her now. Marie, this is my friend Gottfried.

Marie: Hi, Gottfried. Nice to meet you.

Gottfried: You, too. Would you like a drink?

Marie: Sure, let's go get one.

3. Ein Telefonat – A Telephone Call

Hans: Hi Adelheid, hier ist Hans. Wie geht es dir?

Adelheid: Oh, hallo Hans! Ich habe grade an dich gedacht.

Hans: Das ist schön. Ich habe mich gefragt ob du heute Abend ins Kino gehen möchtest?

Adelheid: Ja, das wäre schön! Welchen Film möchtest du sehen?

Hans: Ich dachte an die neue Komödie *Mach das Licht aus*. Was hältst du davon?

Adelheid: Klingt gut!

Hans: Ok, ich hol dich so um 19:30 Uhr ab. Der Film fängt um 20:00 Uhr an.

Adelheid: Bis später, Tschüss!

A TELEPHONE CALL

Hans: Hi, Adelheid, it's Hans. How are you?

Adelheid: Oh, hi, Hans! I was just thinking about you.

Hans: That's nice. I was wondering if you'd like to go to a movie tonight.

Adelheid: Sure, I'd love to! Which movie do you want to see?

Hans: I was thinking about that new comedy *Turn Off the Lights*. What do you think?

Adelheid: Sounds great!

Hans: Ok, I'll pick you up around 7:30. The movie starts at 8:00.

Adelheid: See you then. Bye!

4. WIE VIEL UHR IST ES? – WHAT TIME IS IT?

Natascha: Wie viel Uhr ist es? Wir sind spät dran!

Antonio: Es ist viertel nach Sieben. Wir sind pünktlich. Mach dir keine Sorgen.

Natascha: Aber ich dachte wir müssen um 19:30 Uhr im Restaurant sein, für die Überraschungsparty. Das schaffen wir niemals mit dem ganzen Verkehr am Abend.

Antonio: Ich bin mir sicher wir schaffen es. Berufsverkehr ist fast zu Ende. Die Party fängt sowieso erst um 20:00 Uhr an.

Aber ich brauche Hilfe mit dem Weg. Kannst du das Restaurant anrufen und fragen wo wir unser Auto parken können?

Natascha: Natürlich.

What Time Is It?

Natascha: What time is it? We're going to be late!

Antonio: It's a quarter after seven. We're on time. Don't panic.

Natascha: But I thought we had to be at the restaurant by 7:30 for the surprise party. We'll never make it there with all this evening traffic.

Antonio: I'm sure we will. Rush hour is almost over. Anyway, the party starts at 8:00.

But I do need help with directions. Can you call the restaurant and ask them where we park our car?

Natascha: Of course.

5. KANNST DU DAS NOCHMAL SAGEN? – CAN YOU SAY THAT AGAIN?

Lukas: Hallo? Hi Stefania, wie läuft es im Büro?

Stefania: Hi Lukas! Wie geht es dir? Kannst du bitte beim Supermarkt vorbei fahren und mehr Papier für den Drucker besorgen?

Lukas: Was hast du gesagt? Kannst du das bitte wiederholen? Hast du gesagt ich soll Tinte für den Drucker besorgen? Tut mir leid, ich verstehe nicht alles.

Stefania: Kannst du mich jetzt hören? Nein, ich brauche mehr Papier. Hör zu, ich schicke dir in einer SMS genau was ich brauche. Danke Lukas. Wir hören uns später.

Lukas: Danke Stefania. Tut mir leid, mein Telefon hat keinen guten Empfang hier.

CAN YOU SAY THAT AGAIN?

Lukas: Hello? Hi, Stefania, how are things at the office?

Stefania: Hi, Lukas! How are you? Can you please stop at the store and pick up extra paper for the printer?

Lukas: What did you say? Can you repeat that, please? Did you say to pick up ink for the printer? Sorry, the phone is cutting out.

Stefania: Can you hear me now? No, I need more computer paper. Listen, I'll text you exactly what I need. Thanks, Lukas.

Talk to you later.

Lukas: Thanks, Stefania. Sorry, my phone has really bad

reception here.

6. Zufälle – Coincidences

Margarete: Hallo Julia! Lange nicht gesehen!

Julia: Margarete! Hi! Was für ein Zufall! Ich hab dich ewig nicht mehr gesehen! Was machst du hier?

Margarete: Ich hab einen neuen Arbeitsplatz in der Stadt, also kaufe ich ein paar Klamotten ein. Hey, was hältst du von diesem Oberteil?

Julia: Hmmm.. Du weißt ja wie sehr ich Blau mag. Ich habe das selbe Oberteil!

Margarete: Du hattest immer einen guten Geschmack! Wie klein die Welt doch ist.

COINCIDENCES

Margarete: Well, hello there, Julia! Long time no see!

Julia: Margarete! Hi! What a coincidence! I haven't seen you in forever! What are you doing here?

Margarete: I just got a new job in the city, so I'm shopping for some clothes. Hey, what do you think of this shirt?

Julia: Hmmm... Well, you know how much I love blue. See? I've got the same shirt!

Margarete: You always did have good taste! What a small world.

7. DAS WETTER – THE WEATHER

Sarah: Es ist eiskalt draußen! Was ist mit der Wettervorhersage passiert? Ich dachte die Kaltfront soll vorbei sein.

Gabi: Ja, das dachte ich auch. Das habe ich heute morgen im Internet gelesen.

Sarah: Ich denke, dass der eisige Wind die Temperatur sinken lässt.

Gabi: Können wir rein gehen? Fühlt sich so an als ob meine Zehen taub werden.

The Weather

Sarah: It's freezing outside! What happened to the weather report? I thought this cold front was supposed to pass.

Gabi: Yeah, I thought so too. That's what I read online this morning.

Sarah: I guess the wind chill is really driving down the temperature.

Gabi: Can we go inside? I feel like my toes are starting to go numb.

8. ESSEN BESTELLEN – ORDERING FOOD

Kellner: Hallo, ich bin Ihr Kellner für heute. Kann ich Ihnen was zu trinken bringen?

Hans: Ja. Ich hätte gerne einen Eistee.

Anna: Und ich hätte gerne eine Limonade.

Kellner: Ok sind Sie bereit zu bestellen oder brauchen Sie noch ein paar Minuten?

Hans: Ich denke wir sind soweit. Ich möchte bitte die Tomatensuppe als Vorspeise und dann das Rinderbraten mit Kartoffelpueree und Erbsen.

Kellner: Wie möchten Sie ihr Rindfleisch – roh, medium oder ganz durch.

Hans: Durch bitte.

Anna: Und ich möchte gerne den Fisch mit Kartoffeln und Salat.

Ordering Food

Waiter: Hello, I'll be your waiter today. Can I start you off with something to drink?

Hans: Yes. I would like iced tea, please.

Anna: And I'll have lemonade, please.

Waiter: Ok. Are you ready to order, or do you need a few minutes?

Hans: I think we're ready. I'll have the tomato soup to start, and the roast beef with mashed potatoes and peas.

Waiter: How do you want the beef — rare, medium, or well done?

Hans: Well done, please.

Anna: And I'll just have the fish, with potatoes and a salad.

9. Besuch beim Arzt – Visiting The Doctor

Arzt: Wie kann ich dir helfen?

Catia: Also, ich habe einen schlimmen Husten und Halsschmerzen. Außerdem habe ich Kopfschmerzen.

Arzt: Wie lange hast du diese Symptome schon?

Catia: Ungefähr drei Tage. Ich bin auch sehr müde.

Arzt: Hmm. Klingt nach der Grippe. Nimm alle vier Stunden Aspirin und ruhe dich gut aus. Nimm außerdem genug Flüssigkeit zu dir. Wenn du nächste Woche noch krank bist, dann rufe mich an.

Catia: Ok, Dankeschön.

VISITING THE DOCTOR

Doctor: What seems to be the problem?

Catia: Well... I have a bad cough and a sore throat. I also have a headache.

Doctor: How long have you had these symptoms?

Catia: About three days now. And I'm really tired, too.

Doctor: Hmm. It sounds like you've got the flu. Take aspirin every four hours and get plenty of rest. Make sure you drink lots of fluids. Call me if you're still sick next week.

Catia: Ok, thank you.

10. NACH DEM WEG FRAGEN – ASKING FOR DIRECTIONS

Mark: Entschuldigung. Kannst du mir sagen wo die Bücherei ist?

Vivien: Ja, es ist dort lang. Du gehst drei Blocks in die Washington Straße, dann biegst du rechts ab. Es ist an der Ecke, gegenüber der Bank.

Mark: Danke! Ich bin erst seit ein paar Tagen in der Stadt, also kenne ich mich noch nicht so gut aus.

Vivien: Oh, ich weiß wie du dich fühlst. Wir sind hier vor einem Jahr hergezogen und ich kenne auch noch nicht alles!

ASKING FOR DIRECTIONS

Mark: Excuse me. Could you tell me where the library is?

Vivien: Yes, it's that way. You go three blocks to Washington Street, then turn right. It's on the corner, across from the bank.

Mark: Thanks! I've only been in town a few days, so I really don't know my way around yet.

Vivien: Oh, I know how you feel. We moved here a year ago, and I still don't know where everything is!

11. Nach Hilfe rufen – Calling For Help

Peter: Hey! Dieses Auto ist gerade bei rot durchgefahren und in den Lastwagen geprallt!

Gabi: Ist jemand verletzt?

Peter: Ich weiß es nicht... lass uns den Notruf 911 anrufen... Hallo? Ich möchte einen Unfall in der Nähe vom Postamt in der Houston Straße melden. Es sieht so aus als ob ein Mann verletzt ist. Ja, es ist gerade eben erst passiert. Ok, Danke, Tschüss.

Gabi: Was haben sie gesagt?

Peter: Sie senden sofort einen Krankenwagen und die Polizei.

Gabi: Gut, sie sind hier. Ich hoffe dem Mann geht es gut.

Peter: Ich weiß. Man muss so vorsichtig sein, wenn man Auto fährt.

CALLING FOR HELP

Peter: Hey! That car just ran a red light and hit that truck!

Gabi: Is anyone hurt?

Peter: I don't know... let's call 911. ...Hello? I'd like to report a car accident near the post office on Houston Street. It looks like a man is hurt. Yes, it just happened. Ok, thanks. Bye.

Gabi: What did they say?

Peter: They're going to send an ambulance and a police car right away.

Gabi: Good, they're here. I hope the man is alright.

Peter: I know. You have to be so careful when you're driving.

12. EINKAUFEN – SHOPPING

Luisa: Hey Julia, schau dir diese Nachtische an! Wie wäre es wenn wir heute Kekse backen?

Julia: Hmm.. Ja das ist eine gute Idee! Lass uns alle Zutaten kaufen während wir hier sind. Was brauchen wir?

Luisa: Im Rezept steht Mehl, Zucker und Butter. Oh, und wir brauchen außerdem Eier und Schokoladenraspeln.

Julia: Ich schlage vor dass du die Milchproduckte holst. Du findest sie in der Kühlabteilung im hinteren Ende vom Supermarkt. Ich hole die trockenen Zutaten. Ich glaube die sind in Gang 10.

Luisa: Super! Lass uns an der Kasse treffen.

Julia: Ok, wir sehen uns an der Kasse.

SHOPPING

Luisa: Hey, Julia... Look at those desserts! How about baking some cookies today?

Julia: Hmm... Yeah, that's a great idea! While we're here, let's pick up the ingredients. What do we need?

Luisa: The recipe calls for flour, sugar and butter. Oh, and we also need eggs and chocolate chips.

Julia: Why don't you get the dairy ingredients? You'll find those in the refrigerated section in the back of the store. I'll get the dry ingredients. I believe they're in aisle 10.

Luisa: Great! Let's meet at the checkout.

Julia: Ok. See you there.

13. ERLEDIGUNGEN MACHEN – RUNNING ERRANDS

Hotel Rezeptionist: Hallo, wie kann ich Ihnen helfen?

Klara: Ich bin für ein paar Tage zu Besuch in der Stadt und während ich hier bin muss ich einige Dinge erledigen.

Hotel Rezeptionist: Sicher. Was brauchen Sie?

Klara: Ich muss meine Haare schneiden lassen. Außerdem muss ich meine neue Hose enger nähen lassen.

Hotel Rezeptionist: Ok. Hier ist ein Stadtplan. Hier ist ein guter Friseursalon, nur einen Block entfernt. Und hier ist eine Änderungsschneiderei. Ist da noch etwas dass Sie brauchen?

Klara: Ja. Ich muss mein Auto in die Autowerkstatt bringen bevor ich den langen Weg zurück nach Hause fahre.

Hotel Rezeptionist: Kein Problem. Ein paar Blocks entfernt ist eine gute Autowerkstatt.

RUNNING ERRANDS

Hotel receptionist: Hello there. How can I help you?

Klara: Well, I'm in town visiting for a few days, and I need to get some things done while I'm here.

Hotel receptionist: Sure. What do you need?

Klara: I need to get my hair cut. I also need to have my new pants hemmed.

Hotel receptionist: Ok. Here's a map of the city. There's a good hair salon here, which is just a block away. And there's a tailor right here. Is there anything else?

Klara: Yes. I'll need to get my car serviced before my long drive back home!

Hotel receptionist: No problem. There's a good mechanic a few blocks away.

14. BEIM POSTAMT – AT THE POST OFFICE

Postangestellter: Wie kann ich Ihnen heute helfen?

Carolin: Ich möchte bitte dieses Paket nach New York verschicken.

Postangestellter: Ok, mal schauen wie viel es wiegt... es wiegt ungefähr fünf Pfund. Wenn Sie den Expressversand möchten, dann kommt es morgen an. Oder sie können den Versand mit Priorität wählen, dann kommt es bis Samstag an.

Carolin: Samstag ist in Ordnung. Wie viel kostet das?

Postangestellter: €12.41. Brauchen Sie noch etwas anderes?

Carolin: Oh ja! Hab ich fast vergessen. Ich brauche bitte ein Briefmarkenset.

Postangestellter: Ok, das macht insgesamt bitte €18.94.

AT THE POST OFFICE

Postal clerk: How can I help you today?

Carolin: I need to mail this package to New York, please.

Postal clerk: Ok, let's see how much it weighs... it's about five pounds. If you send it express, it will get there tomorrow. Or you can send it priority and it will get there by Saturday.

Carolin: Saturday is fine. How much will that be?

Postal clerk: €12.41. Do you need anything else?

Carolin: Oh, yeah! I almost forgot. I need a book of stamps, too.

Postal clerk: Ok, your total comes to €18.94.

15. DIE PRÜFUNG – THE EXAM

Charlotte: Hey! Wie lief es in deiner Physik Prüfung?

Frank: Nicht schlecht, danke. Ich bin nur froh das es vorbei ist! Wie war es bei dir.. wie lief deine Präsentation?

Charlotte: Oh, es lief sehr gut. Danke für deine Hilfe!

Frank: Kein Problem. Also... was hältst du davon morgen zusammen für unsere Matheprüfung zu lernen?

Charlotte: Ja sicher! Komm nach dem Frühstück so um 10:00 Uhr zu mir.

Frank: In Ordnung, Ich bringe meine Notizen mit.

CATCHING UP

Charlotte: Hey! How did your physics exam go?

Frank: Not bad, thanks. I'm just glad it's over! How about you... how'd your presentation go?

Charlotte: Oh, it went really well. Thanks for helping me with it!

Frank: No problem. So... do you feel like studying tomorrow for our math exam?

Charlotte: Yeah, sure! Come over around 10:00 am, after breakfast.

Frank: Alright. I'll bring my notes.

16. DER PERFEKTE PULLOVER – THE PERFECT SWEATER

Verkäufer: Kann ich helfen?

Gloria: Ja, ich suche nach einem Pullover- in der Größe Medium.

Verkäufer: Mal sehen..hier haben wir einen schönen in weiß. Was hältst du von dem?

Gloria: Ich denke ich bevorzuge blau.

Verkäufer: Ok... hier haben wir blau in Medium. Würdest du den gerne anprobieren?

Gloria: Ok... Ja, ich liebe es. Passt perfekt. Wie viel kostet der?

Verkäufer: Der kostet €41. Mit Steuern macht das €50.

Gloria: Perfekt! Den nehme ich! Dankeschön!

THE PERFECT SWEATER

Salesperson: Can I help you?

Gloria: Yes, I'm looking for a sweater — in a size medium.

Salesperson: Let's see... here's a nice white one. What do you think?

Gloria: I think I'd rather have it in blue.

Salesperson: Ok ... here's blue, in a medium. Would you like to try it on?

Gloria: Ok ... yes, I love it. It fits perfectly. How much is it?

Salesperson: It's €41. It will be €50, with tax.

Gloria: Perfect! I'll take it. Thank you!

17. Taxi oder Bus – Taxi Or Bus

Johanna: Sollen wir mit dem Taxi oder mit dem Bus ins Kino fahren?

Ben: Lass uns den Bus nehmen. Es ist unmöglich ein Taxi während dem Berufsverkehr zu bekommen.

Johanna: Ist das nicht eine Bushaltestelle dort drüben?

Ben: Ja.. Oh! Da kommt ein Bus. Wir müssen rennen um ihn zu schaffen.

Johanna: Oh nein! Wir haben ihn gerade verpasst.

Ben: Kein Problem. Der nächste kommt in 10 Minuten.

TAXI OR BUS

Johanna: Should we take a taxi or a bus to the movie theater?

Ben: Let's take a bus. It's impossible to get a taxi during rush hour.

Johanna: Isn't that a bus stop over there?

Ben: Yes... Oh! There's a bus now. We'll have to run to catch it.

Johanna: Oh, no! We just missed it.

Ben: No problem. There'll be another one in 10 minutes.

18. WIE ALT BIST DU? – HOW OLD ARE YOU?

Gloria: Ich freue mich schon sehr auf Tante Marie's Geburtstag's Überraschungsparty heute Nachmittag. Du dich auch?

Nadine: Ja! Wie alt ist sie?

Gloria: Sie wird am 5. Mai 55.

Nadine: Wow! Ich wusste gar nicht, dass meine Mutter älter ist – sie wird am 9. Oktober 58. Wie auch immer, Tante Marie wird so überrascht sein uns alle zu sehen!

Gloria: Ich weiß! Aber wir müssen immer noch das ganze Essen vorbereiten bevor sie hier ist..ok! Wir sind alle fertig! Shh! Hier kommt sie!

Alle: Überraschung!

HOW OLD ARE YOU?

Gloria: I'm really excited for Aunt Marie's surprise birthday party this afternoon! Aren't you?

Nadine: Yeah! How old is she?

Gloria: She'll be 55 on May 5.

Nadine: Wow! I didn't know that my mom was older — she's going to be 58 on October 9. Anyway, Aunt Marie's going to be so surprised to see us all here!

Gloria: I know! But we still have to get all the food set up before she gets here ... Ok! We're all ready now. Shh! She's here!

All: Surprise!

19. Im Kino – At The Theater

Bernd: Wir möchten bitte zwei Karten für die Vorstellung um 3:30.

Kartenverkäufer: Hier bitte. Viel Spaß beim Film!

(Im Kino)

Bernd: Macht es Ihnen etwas aus einen Sitz weiter zu rutschen damit mein Freund und ich zusammen sitzen können.

Frau: Nein, natürlich nicht.

Bernd: Vielen Dank!

At The Theater

Bernd: We'd like two tickets for the 3:30 show, please.

Ticket sales: Here you go. Enjoy the movie!

[Inside the theater]

Bernd: Would you mind moving over one, so my friend and I can sit together?

Woman: No, not at all.

Bernd: Thank you so much!

20. WORIN BIST DU GUT? – WHAT ARE YOU GOOD AT DOING?

Sandra: Also, was sollen wir machen?

Pamela: Also, ich mag Basteln gerne und ich bin sehr gut im Zeichnen. Was denkst du?

Sandra: Hmm.. Wie wäre es mit einem Brettspiel? Das macht mehr Spaß.

Pamela: Ok. Lass uns Scrabble spielen! Ich bin auch sehr gut im Buchstabieren!

Sandra: Oh ja? Wir werden sehen!

WHAT ARE YOU GOOD AT DOING?

Sandra: So ... what should we do?

Pamela: Well, I like to do arts and crafts, and I'm really good at drawing. What do you think?

Sandra: Hmm ... how about playing a board game? That would be more fun.

Pamela: Ok. Let's play Scrabble! I'm really good at spelling, too!

Sandra: Oh, yeah? We'll see about that!

21. WAS IST DEIN LIEBLINGSPORT? – WHAT IS YOUR FAVORITE SPORT?

Philip: Um wie viel Uhr ist das Fußballspiel? Ich dachte es fängt um 12:00 Uhr an?

Jan: Wir müssen die falsche Uhrzeit haben. Oh... na ja Fußball ist sowieso nicht mein Lieblingssport. Ich mag Basketball lieber.

Philip: Oh wirklich? Ich dachte dein Lieblingssport ist Tennis? Ich bin auch ein großer Fan von Basketball.

Jan: Wie wäre es mal mit einem Spiel?

Philip: Ja sicher! Wieso werfen wir nicht jetzt ein paar Körbe jetzt wo das Fußballspiel eh nicht ist?

Jan: Ausgezeichnete Idee! Los geht's.

What Is Your Favorite Sport?

Philip: What time is that soccer game on? I thought it started at noon.

Jan: We must have had the wrong time. Oh, well ... soccer's not my favorite sport anyway. I much prefer basketball.

Philip: Oh, really? I thought your favorite sport was tennis! I'm a big fan of basketball, too.

Jan: How about a game sometime?

Philip: Sure thing! Why don't we go shoot some hoops now since the soccer game isn't on?

Jan: Excellent idea. Let's go.

22. Ein Musical ansehen – Going To See A Musical

Sarah: Was für eine fantastische Vorstellung! Danke für die Einladung zum Musical!

Elena: Bitteschön. Ich freue mich dass es dir gefallen hat. Die Choreographie der Tänzer war unglaublich. Das erinnert mich an die Zeit als ich vor vielen Jahren getanzt habe.

Sarah: Ich weiß! Du warst so eine talentierte Ballerina. Vermisst du es zu tanzen?

Elena: Oh, das ist sehr nett von dir Sara. Ja manchmal vermisse ich es. Aber ich werde immer ein Fan von der Kunst zu tanzen sein. Das ist der Grund für meine Begeisterung für Musicals. Es ist die perfekte Kombination von Tanz, Gesang und Theater.

Sarah: Absolut! Ich bin froh dass du immer noch ein Fan davon bist. Danke für die Einladung. Es ist immer ein Vergnügen mit dir Vorstellungen zu besuchen und etwas neues zu lernen.

GOING TO SEE A MUSICAL

Sarah: What a fantastic performance! Thank you for inviting me to the musical.

Elena: You are welcome. I'm happy you enjoyed the show. The choreography of the dancers was incredible. It reminds me of when I used to dance many years ago.

Sarah: I know! You were such a talented ballerina. Do you miss dancing?

Elena: Oh, that's very kind of you, Sarah. I do miss it sometimes. But I will always be a fan of the arts. That's why I love going to musicals because it's the perfect combination of dance, song and theater.

Sarah: Absolutely! I'm glad you are still an art fan too. Thank you for the invitation. It's always a pleasure to attend an arts event with you and learn something new.

23. Im Urlaub – Taking A Vacation

Gemma: Ich habe gerade ein Flugticket nach New York City gekauft. Ich bin so aufgeregt die Stadt zu sehen!

Sophia: Gut für dich! Reisen macht so viel Spaß. Ich liebe es neue Plätze und Leute zu entdecken. Wann fliegst du denn?

Gemma: Nächste Woche. Ich nehme den Flug der in der Nacht losfliegt und am Morgen ankommt. Das war günstiger. Hoffentlich kann ich im Flugzeug schlafen.

Sophia: Ich wünschte ich könnte mitkommen! New York City ist ein magischer Platz. Du wirst so viel Spaß haben.

Gemma: Ich hoffe es. Ich werde meinen Bruder besuchen, der lebt dort. Ich bleibe dort für eine Woche und fahre dann mit dem Zug nach Washington DC.

Sophia: Das klingt nach einem tollen Urlaub. Ich freue mich schon auf eine Woche Strand in meinem Sommerurlaub. Ich will einfach nur entspannen.

TAKING A VACATION

Gemma: I just bought a ticket to New York City. I'm so excited to see the city!

Sophia: Good for you! Traveling is so much fun. I love discovering new places and new people. When are you leaving?

Gemma: Next week. I'm taking the red eye. It was cheaper. Hopefully, I'll be able to sleep on the plane.

Sophia: I wish I could go with you! New York City is a magical place. You will have so much fun.

Gemma: I hope so. I'm going to visit my brother who lives there. I will stay for a week and then take the train down to Washington, DC

Sophia: That sounds like a great vacation. I'm looking forward to a week at the beach for my summer vacation. I just want to relax.

24. Im Tierhandel – At The Pet Store

Corinna: Was für eine wunderschöne Katze! Was denkst du?

Hans: Ich glaube ich hätte lieber einen Hund. Hunde sind loyaler als Katzen. Katzen sind nur faul.

Corinna: Ja, aber Hunde brauchen viel mehr Aufmerksamkeit! Wärst du bereit jeden Tag spazieren zu gehen und hinter dem Hund sauber zu machen?

Hans: Hmm. Ja das ist ein guter Punkt. Wie wäre es mit einem Vogel? Oder einem Fisch?

Corinna: Wir würden eine Menge Geld in den Käfig oder ein Aquarium investieren. Und ehrlich gesagt weiß ich gar nicht wie man sich um einen Vogel oder einen Fisch kümmert.

Hans: Wir sind offensichtlich noch nicht bereit für ein Haustier.

Corinna: Haha.. Ja, du hast Recht. Lass uns Essen gehen und darüber reden.

AT THE PET STORE

Corinna: What a beautiful cat! What do you think?

Hans: I think I'd rather get a dog. Dogs are more loyal than cats. Cats are just lazy.

Corinna: Yes, but they need so much attention! Would you be willing to walk it every single day? And clean up after it?

Hans: Hmm. Good point. What about a bird? Or a fish?

Corinna: We'd have to invest a lot of money in a cage or a fish tank. And I honestly don't know how to take care of a bird or a fish!

Hans: Well, we're obviously not ready to get a pet yet.

Corinna: Haha... Yeah, you're right. Let's get some food and talk about it.

25. Deine Meinung Äussern – Expressing Your Opinion

Walter: Wo sollen wir dieses Jahr Urlaub machen? Wir müssen uns bald entscheiden.

Mia: Also ich würde gerne irgendwo hin wo es warm ist. Wie wäre es mit dem Strand? Oder wir könnten eine Hütte am See mieten.

Walter: Du willst schon wieder an den Strand? Ich will diesen Winter Ski fahren. Wir können einen Kompromiss finden und im April in die Rocky Mountains nach Colorado fliegen? Dort gibt es wunderschöne Skiorte.

Mia: Oh, wir waren noch nie in Colorado! Aber ich weiß nicht ob es dann auch warm und sonnig ist? Ich muss mich zuerst erkundigen. Das hilft mir eine Entscheidung zu treffen.

EXPRESSING YOUR OPINION

Walter: Where should we take a vacation this year? We need to decide soon.

Mia: Well, I'd like to go somewhere warm. How about the beach? Or we could rent a cabin on the lake.

Walter: You want to go to the beach, again? I want to ski this winter. We can compromise and travel to the Rocky Mountains in Colorado next April? There are beautiful ski resorts there.

Mia: Oh, we've never been to Colorado before! But I don't know if it will be sunny and warm then. I need to do some research first. That will help me make a decision.

26. HOBBIES – HOBBIES

Rolf: Ich freue mich so dass diese Woche die Prüfungen zu ende sind.

Tom: Ja ich auch. Ich freue mich schon so auf Entspannung in den Bergen dieses Wochenende. Ich habe eine kleine Wanderung in den Wäldern geplant. Und, wenn das Wetter gut ist, will ich mit dem Kanu den Fluss entlang.

Rolf: Oh das klingt nach Spaß! Ich reise nach Colorado. Ich nehme meine Kamera mit, der Herbst kommt schnell. Die Blätter färben sich schon in viel verschiedene Rot und Orange Töne. Das wird großartig.

Tom: Das nächste Mal wenn du gehst, komme ich mit dir. Ich habe gehört, dass Colorado ein großartiger Platz zum Kanu fahren ist.

HOBBIES

Rolf: I'm so happy this week of midterm exams is finished.

Tom: Same here. I'm looking forward to relaxing in the mountains this weekend. I've planned a nice little hike in the woods. Also, if the weather is good, I'm going to go canoeing down the river.

Rolf: Oh, how fun! I'm going to Colorado. I'm taking my camera because fall is coming fast. The leaves are already turning shades of red and orange. It will be awesome.

Tom: Next time you go there, I'll join you. I've heard Colorado is a great place to go canoeing.

27. Die Hochzeit – The Wedding

Angelika: Sieht die Braut nicht wunderschön aus in ihrem Hochzeitskleid?

Maria: Ja. Sie sieht toll aus. Und der Bräutigam ist so romantisch.

Ich habe gerade gehört wie sie sich verlobt haben. Er hat ihr einen Antrag während einem Abendessen bei Kerzenschein in Prag gemacht. Dort sind sie zur Schule gegangen.

Angelika: Oh ja? Wunderbar. Und die Hochzeitsreise! Was für eine großartige Idee! Die meisten machen Strandurlaub für eine Woche nachdem sie den Bund fürs Leben geschlossen haben. Ich finde das so eine langweilige Idee. Stattdessen planen sie in Kalifornien an der Küste mit ihren Motorrädern entlang zu fahren.

Maria: Wirklich! Was für eine fantastische Idee. Das ist bei weitem die beste Hochzeit auf der ich je war!

THE WEDDING

Angelika: Doesn't the bride look beautiful in that wedding dress?

Maria: Yes. She looks amazing. And the groom is such a romantic.

I just heard the story of how they got engaged! He proposed to her during a candlelight dinner in Prague. That was where they went to school.

Angelika: Oh yea? Wonderful. And the honeymoon! What a great idea! Most people just go to the beach for a week after they tie the knot. I think that's such a boring idea. Instead, they plan on going to California and cruising the coast on their motorcycle.

Maria: Really! What a fantastic idea. This is by far the best wedding I've ever been to in my life!

28. Einen Ratschlag geben – Giving Advice

Lea: Danke dass du dich während deiner Mittagspause mit mir triffst. Ich schätze das sehr.

Monika: Kein Problem. Ich bin froh wenn ich dir helfen kann. Was ist den passiert?

Lea: Ach du weißt schon, das Übliche. Ich muss mich bald entscheiden.. Soll ich den neuen Job annehmen? Oder soll ich lieber in meinem jetzigen bleiben?

Monika: Also, ich denke, dass es Zeit für eine Veränderung ist, denkst du nicht? Sie bezahlen dich zu spät und du bist nicht glücklich. Das sind mehr als genug Gründe einen Job zu kündigen.

Lea: Denkst du wirklich?

Monika: Ich weiß es. Und ich habe deinen Beschwerden jetzt über ein Jahr zugehört. Vertrau mir. Nimm den Job. Was hast du zu verlieren?

Lea: Ok, du hast mich überzeugt. Du gibst mir immer die richtigen Ratschläge.

GIVING ADVICE

Lea: Thanks for meeting with me during your lunch hour. I appreciate it.

Monika: No problem. I'm happy to help. What's happening?

Lea: Oh you know, the usual. I have to decide soon... Should I take this new job? Or do I stick with my current one?

Monika: Well, I think it's time for a change, don't you? They pay you late and you are unhappy. That's more than enough reasons to quit your job.

Lea: Do you really think so?

Monika: I know so. And I've been listening to you complain for over a year now. Trust me. Take the job. What do you have to lose?

Lea: Ok, you convinced me. You have always given me the best advice.

29. Kinder unterrichten – Teaching Children

Samuel: Hallo Otto, wie war dein Tag?

Otto: Hi Samuel, wo warst du? Ich habe nach dir gesucht.

Samuel: Du wirst mir nicht glauben was für eine interessante Erfahrung ich gemacht habe. Ich habe den ganzen Tag mit einer Menge Kindern verbracht!

Otto: Das klingt nach Spaß. Erzähl mir mehr.

Samuel: Ja, ich hatte eine großartige Zeit.. aber es war sehr anstrengend! Ich habe nicht gewusst, dass Kinder so viel Energie haben.

Otto: Wo hast du all diese Kinder getroffen?

Samuel: In der Grundschule in Chicago. Ich hatte die Möglichkeit am morgen einige Unterrichtsstunden zu besuchen. Danach, am Nachmittag, habe ich ihnen einfaches Englisch beigebracht, mit einigen Wortspielen.

Otto: Ich bin sicher Englisch war bestimmt sehr schwer für sie.

Samuel: Überraschender weise waren alle sehr begierig zu lernen. Ehrlich, ich war sehr beeindruckt.

Otto: Das ist gut. Was hast du denn unterrichtet?

Samuel: Die Kinder lieben es alles laut zu wiederholen! Manchmal habe ich den Satz laut gerufen und sie haben zurück gerufen. Ich habe geflüstert und sie haben zurück geflüstert. Es hat so viel Spaß gemacht!

Otto: Weißt du, als ich ein Austauschschüler war, hatten wir nie solche Englisch Stunden. Es freut mich sehr, dass die Kinder so eine wunderbare Erfahrung hatten.

TEACHING CHILDREN

Samuel: Hi Otto, how was your day?

Otto: Hi Samuel, where have you been? I've been looking for you.

Samuel: You won't believe the interesting experience I just had. I spent the whole day with a ton of children!

Otto: That sounds like fun. Tell me more.

Samuel: Yes, it was a great time... but it was so exhausting! I didn't realize that kids have so much energy.

Otto: Where did you meet all these kids?

Samuel: At the elementary school in Chicago. I had an opportunity to visit some of their classes in the morning. After that I taught them some basic English with word games in the afternoon.

Otto: I'm sure English was probably very difficult for them.

Samuel: Surprisingly, they were all very eager to learn. Honestly, I was impressed.

Otto: That's great. What did you end up teaching them?

Samuel: The kids love to repeat things out loud! Sometimes I yelled out the sentences, and they yelled back at me. I whispered, and they whispered back. It was so much fun!

Otto: You know, when I was a foreign exchange student, we never had English lessons like that. It makes me happy the children had such a wonderful experience.

30. Spass mit Tennis – Fun With Tennis

Anna: Sebastian, kannst du mit bitte zeigen wie man den Schläger hält?

Sebastian: Klar Anna, es ist so als würden wir Hände schütteln. Halte deine Hand als würdest du meine Hand schütteln.

Anna: So?

Sebastian: Ja genau so. Jetzt halte so den Schläger in deiner Hand.

Anna: Jetzt bin ich bereit den Ball wie ein Profi zu schlagen!

Sebastian: Haha, fast! Erinnere dich daran, was ich dir erzählt habe. Es gibt nur zwei Arten von Schwüngen, die Vorhand und die Rückhand.

Anna: Ok, ich erinnere mich. Du hast gesagt mit der Vorhand den Ball treffen ist wie einen Tischtennisball schlagen.

Sebastian: Das ist richtig. Versuche es mal. Bist du bereit? Triff den!

Anna: Ups! Den habe ich komplett verpasst!

Sebastian: Das ist in Ordnung, versuche es nochmal.

Anna: Oh ich sehe. Lass es mich nochmal versuchen..

Sebastian: Hier kommt noch ein Ball.. Wow! Du hast ihn über das Netz geschlagen. Du bist eine sehr starke Dame.

Anna: Haha. Ich glaube ich muss mehr üben!

Fun With Tennis

Anna: Sebastian, could you show me how to hold the racket?

Sebastian: Sure Anna, it's just like when we shake hands. Hold your hand out as if you were about to shake my hand...

Anna: Just like this?

Sebastian: Yes, just like that. Now, put the racket in your hand, like this.

Anna: Now I'm ready to hit the ball like a professional!

Sebastian: Haha, almost! Remember what I told you. There are only two types of swings, the forehand and the backhand.

Anna: Ok, I remember. You said hitting a forehand, starting on my right, is like hitting a ping pong ball.

Sebastian: That's right. Give it a try now. Are you ready? Hit this!

Anna: Oops! I completely missed it!

Sebastian: That's alright, try again.

Anna: Oh, I see. Let me try again...

Sebastian: Here comes another ball... Wow! You hit it over the fence! You're a very powerful lady.

Anna: Haha. I guess I need to practice more!

31. Leben in Kalifornien – Living In California

Jessika: Es ist so kalt heute Morgen.

Tatjana: Ja es ist kalt. Heute Morgen musste ich meine Windschutzscheibe am Auto einsprühen weil sie eingefroren war.

Jessika: Ich hätte nie gedacht, dass es Anfang Dezember so kalt sein würde, vor allem in Kalifornien.

Tatjana: Ich weiß. Die Temperatur war 40 Grad Fahrenheit heute Morgen als ich aufgewacht bin. Ich habe gefroren sobald ich aus dem Bett aufgestanden bin. Das kalte Wetter war definitiv keine schöne Überraschung.

Jessika: Ich kann mich nicht erinnern ob es tatsächlich im Dezember schon mal so kalt war.

Tatjana: Was noch schlimmer ist, es soll am Nachmittag regnen. Es wird kalt und nass sein!

Jessika: Iiih! Es regnet am Nachmittag?

Tatjana: Nicht nur am Nachmittag, sondern auch die ganze restliche Woche. Die Nachrichten haben gesagt es fängt um kurz vor 12 Uhr an zu nieseln und dann bis 16 Uhr wird es immer stärker.

Jessika: Ich schätze da ist keine Aussicht auf besseres Wetter diese Woche?

Tatjana: Es gibt einen kleinen Schimmer an Hoffnung das es bis Samstag wieder sonnig ist. Wie auch immer, es wird nebelig, windig und regnerisch sein bevor die Sonne rauskommt.

Jessika: Ich bin froh dass es regnet auch wenn ich Regenwetter nicht mag. Wir hatten eine sehr trockene Zeit bis jetzt.

Tatjana: Ja, ich kann mich kaum erinnern wann es das letzte Mal geregnet hat. Also, solange es kein Gewitter gibt, halte ich es aus.

Jessika: Wir haben kaum Gewitter in Kalifornien.

Tatjana: Wir haben echt Glück, dass Kalifornien eines der besten Wetter in Amerika hat.

Jessika: Du hast Recht, es gibt schlimmere Orte zu leben. Ok, mein Kurs fängt jetzt an. Wir sehen uns später.

Tatjana: Bis später.

LIVING IN CALIFORNIA

Jessica: It is so chilly this morning.

Tatjana: It certainly is. Early this morning I had to spray my car's windshield because it was covered with frost.

Jessica: I never would have thought it could be this cold in early December, especially in California.

Tatjana: I know. The temperature was 40 degrees Fahrenheit when I woke up this morning. I was freezing as soon as I got out of bed. The cold weather was definitely not a nice surprise.

Jessica: I can't remember when it was actually this cold in December.

Tatjana: What's worse is that it's going to rain this afternoon. It's going to be cold and wet!

Jessica: Yuck! It's going to rain this afternoon?

Tatjana: Not just this afternoon, but also the entire rest of the week. The news said that it would start to drizzle just before noon, and then it would rain really hard by four o'clock.

Jessica: I'm guessing there's no sign of better weather this week?

Tatjana: There is a slim chance of sunshine by Saturday. However, it will be foggy, windy, and rainy before the sun comes out this weekend.

Jessica: I am glad that it rains even though I do not like rainy weather. We have a very dry season so far this year.

Tatjana: Yes, I can hardly remember when it rained last time. Well, as long as there is no thunder or lightning, I can stand it.

Jessica: We rarely have thunder or lightning in California.

Tatjana: We are very lucky that California has one of the best weather conditions in America.

Jessica: You are right, there are worse places we could be living. Alright, class is starting right now so I'll see you later.

Tatjana: See you later.

32. Backen – Baking

Charlotte: Mama, was kochst du da? Es riecht so gut.

Frau Müller: Ich backe einen Kuchen. Das ist dein Lieblingskuchen, Karottenkuchen.

Charlotte: Es sieht lecker aus. Und ich sehe auch Muffins da drüben. Du warst beschäftigt, nicht war?

Frau Müller: Ja, Daniel muss morgen welche zu einer Geburtstagsparty bringen. Also diese Muffins sind nur für ihn. Nicht essen.

Charlotte: Kann ich ein Stück vom Kartottenkuchen haben? Ich möchte es jetzt genießen.

Frau Müller: Willst du nicht bis nach dem Abendessen warten?

Charlotte: Der Kuchen ruft meinen Namen, „Charlotte, iss mich.. iss mich.." Nein ich möchte nicht warten. Darf ich Mama?

Frau Müller: Haha.. ok, du darfst.

Charlotte: Lecker! Also was gibt es zum Abendessen?

Frau Müller: Ich mache Rindfleisch und Pilzrahmsuppe.

Charlotte: Du hast lange keine Pilzrahmsuppe mehr gemacht. Brauchst du Hilfe Mama?

Frau Müller: Nein, mach deine Hausaufgaben und überlasse mir das Kochen.

Charlotte: Danke Mama. Ruf mich wenn das Essen fertig ist. Ich möchte nicht zu spät kommen wenn es Rindfleisch, Pilzrahmsuppe, Karottenkuchen und Muffins gibt.

Frau Müller: Die Muffins sind für Daniel. Nicht anfassen!

Charlotte: Ich weiß Mama, ich mache nur Witze.

BAKING

Charlotte: Mom, what are you cooking? It smells so good.

Mrs. Müller: I am baking cakes. This is your favorite carrot cake.

Charlotte: It looks scrumptious. And I see muffins some over there too. You have been busy, haven't you?

Mrs. Müller: Yes. Daniel has to take some to a birthday party tomorrow. So, those muffins are just for him. Don't eat them.

Charlotte: Can I have a piece of carrot cake? I want to enjoy life right now.

Mrs. Müller: You don't want to wait until after dinner?

Charlotte: The cake is calling my name, "Charlotte, eat me... eat me..." No, I don't want to wait. Can I, mom?

Mrs. Müller: Ha ha... Ok, go ahead.

Charlotte: Yum! So what's for dinner tonight?

Mrs. Müller: I will make roast beef and cream of mushroom soup.

Charlotte: It has been a long time since you made cream of mushroom soup. Do you need any help, mom?

Mrs. Müller: No, go do your homework and leave the cooking to me.

Charlotte: Thanks, mom. Call me whenever dinner is ready. I do not want to be late for roast beef, cream of mushroom soup, carrot cake and muffins.

Mrs. Müller: The muffins are for Daniel. Do not touch them!

Charlotte: I know, mom. I'm just kidding.

33. Hilfe übers Telefon – Help Over The Phone

Gabi: Danke für Ihren Anruf beim Sport und Freizeitzentrum. Wie kann ich Ihnen helfen?

Klara: Ich habe vor ein paar Monaten ein Trainingsfahrrad bei Ihnen im Laden gekauft und ich habe jetzt Probleme damit. Es funktioniert nicht mehr und ich hätte es gerne repariert.

Gabi: Ich verbinde sie mit unserem Kundenservice. Einen Moment bitte.

Angelika: Kundenservice, Angelika hier. Wie kann ich Ihnen helfen?

Klara: Ich habe letztes Jahr ein Trainingsfahrrad vom Sportzentrum gekauft und ich hätte es gerne repariert.

Angelika: Was ist das Problem mit dem Fahrrad?

Klara: Ich weiß nicht was passiert ist, aber der Computerbildschirm ist schwarz und geht nicht mehr an.

Angelika: Haben Sie versucht den Start Knopf zu drücken?

Klara: Ja aber nichts passiert.

Angelika: Welches Modell ist das Fahrrad?

Klara: Es ist das Modell Skull Crusher 420Z+, es ist das mit dem coolen Korb vorne dran.

Angelika: Ich kann einen Elektriker vorbeischicken der sich das mal anschaut. Das kostet €5000 und wenn Teile ersetzt werden müssen muss dafür extra bezahlt werden. Klingt das gut?

Klara: Das ist sehr teuer. Ist die Reparatur nicht in der Garantie inbegriffen?

Angelika: Wann haben Sie denn das Fahrrad gekauft?

Klara: Ungefähr vor 3 Monaten.

Angelika: Das tut mir leid. Die Standard Garantie hält nur für einen Monat. Haben Sie extra Garantie gekauft als Sie das Fahrrad gekauft haben?

Klara: Nein, habe ich nicht. Gibt es noch eine andere Möglichkeit außer €5000 für die Reparatur zu zahlen?

Angelika: Nein, leider nicht.

Klara: Das ist verrückt!

Help Over The Phone

Gabi: Thank you for calling Sports Recreation Center. How may I help you?

Klara: I purchased an exercise bike from your store a couple months ago, and I am having problems with it. It stopped working and I need to have it repaired.

Gabi: Let me connect you to the Service department. One moment please.

Angelika: Service department, this is Angelika. How can I help you?

Klara: I bought an exercise bike from Sports Center last year and it needs to be repaired.

Angelika: What seems to be the problem?

Klara: I am not what happened, but the computer screen is black and doesn't turn on anymore.

Angelika: Did you try to press the Start button?

Klara: Yes, and nothing turns on.

Angelika: What is your bike model?

Klara: It is a Skull Crusher 420Z+, it's the one with the really cool basket in the front.

Angelika: I can send a technician out to take a look at your bike. It will cost €5,000.00 for labor. Also, if we have to replace any parts, that will be extra. Sound like a deal?

Klara: That is expensive. Isn't the repair cost covered by warranty?

Angelika: When did you purchase your bike?

Klara: About 3 months ago.

Angelika: I am sorry. The standard warranty only covers 1 month. Did you buy extra warranty coverage at the time of purchase?

Klara: No, I did not. Are there any other options besides paying €5,000.00 for repair labor?

Angelika: No, I am afraid not.

Klara: That's crazy!

34. LASST UNS ZU EINEM KONZERT GEHEN – LET'S GO TO A CONCERT

Karl: Hey Daniela und Simon, heute Abend ist im Park ein Konzert mit guten Bands. Wollt ihr hingehen?

Daniela: Ich arbeite heute Abend nicht, also ich kann auf jeden Fall gehen.

Simon: Ich auch, lasst uns gehen!

Daniela: Es sind so viele Autos unterwegs..

Simon: Ja, wieso ist der Verkehr so schlimm?

Karl: Die Leute fahren bestimmt alle in den Park zu dem Konzert. Es ist eine sehr bekannte Band und die Musik ist sehr gut.

Daniela: Ja sie sind sehr gut. Die letzten vier Jahre habe ich kein einziges Konzert verpasst. Jedes mal wenn die Band in die Stadt kommt kaufe ich sofort ein Ticket.

Simon: Wann hat die Band angefangen hier zu spielen?

Daniela: Sie haben vor 6 Jahren angefangen hier zu spielen und jetzt ist es eine Tradition und sie spielen jedes Jahr die erste Woche im Juni.

Karl: Simon, du wirst den Abend wirklich genießen. Es gibt gute Musik, es wird viel rumgesprungen und definitiv viel Geschrei. Sie haben vielleicht auch eine Tanzfläche zum Moshen.

Simon: Ich kann es kaum abwarten, klingt nach viel Spaß.

Daniela: Mein Lieblingsmusik ist Gangster Rap Musik. Aber ich muss sagen das Country Musik auch sehr angenehmen ist. Überraschender Weise kann ich das den ganzen Tag hören.

Karl: Simon, was für eine Musikrichtung gefällt dir?

Simon: Oh, ich mag alle Musikrichtungen, solange es nicht aggressiv ist.

Daniela: Wow, das Stadion ist voller Menschen! Ich bin überrascht, dass schon so viele Leute für das Konzert hier sind. Gut dass wir auch schon hier sind!

LET'S GO TO A CONCERT

Karl: Hey Daniela, Simon, there is a concert in the park tonight with a great line up. Do you want to go?

Daniela: I don't work tonight so I can definitely go.

Simon: Me too, let's go!

Daniela: There's a ton of cars out tonight...

Simon: Yea, why is the traffic so heavy?

Karl: People are probably heading toward the park for the concert. It's a very popular band and they play really good music.

Daniela: Yes, they do. For the last four years, I have never missed one of their concerts. Every time I find out that the band is coming to town I buy a ticket right away.

Simon: How long ago did the band start playing here locally?

Daniela: They started a tradition six years ago and now every year they play the whole first week of June.

Karl: Simon, you are really going to enjoy this evening. There will be great music, a lot of jumping around, and definitely a lot of shouting. They may even have a mosh pit.

Simon: I can't wait, it sounds like a lot fun.

Daniela: My favorite is gangster rap music; however, I have to say that country music can be pleasant to listen to. Surprisingly, I can listen to it all day long.

Karl: Simon, what kind of music do you like?

Simon: Oh, I like all kinds of music as long as it is not aggressive.

Daniela: Wow, the stadium is packed with people! I'm surprised at the number of people who have already shown up for the concert. It's a good thing we're here already!

35. Pläne machen – Making Plans

Corinna: Lisa, erzähl mal, was hast du für das kommende Wochenende geplant?

Lisa: Ich weiß es nicht. Willst du was gemeinsam unternehmen?

Sarah: Wie wäre es wenn wir einen Film ansehen? AMC 24 in der Parker Straße zeigt, "If You Leave Me, I Delete You."

Corinna: Den wollte ich sehen! Es ist als ob du meine Gedanken lesen würdest. Wollt ihr davor Abendessen gehen?

Sarah: Ja, ist in Ordnung für mich. Wo wollt ihr euch treffen?

Lisa: Lass uns am Red Rooster Haus treffen. Ich war da schon lange nicht mehr.

Corinna: Wieder Mal eine gute Idee. Ich habe gehört, dass die neue Nudelgerichte haben. Es sollte gut sein, Red Rooster Haus hat immer das Beste italienische Essen in der Stadt.

Sarah: Wann sollen wir uns treffen?

Lisa: Also, der Film läuft um 13 Uhr um 14 Uhr um 16 Uhr und um 18 Uhr.

Corinna: Wieso gehen wir nicht zu der Vorstellung um 16 Uhr? Wir können uns um 13 Uhr am Red Rooster Haus treffen, dann haben wir genug Zeit.

MAKING PLANS

Corinna: Lisa, tell me... What are your plans for this upcoming weekend?

Lisa: I don't know. Do you want to get together and do something?

Sarah: How do you feel about going to see a movie? AMC 24 on Parker Road is showing *If You Leave Me, I Delete You.*

Corinna: I've been wanting to see that! It's like you read my mind. Do you want to go out to dinner beforehand?

Sarah: That's fine with me. Where do you want to meet?

Lisa: Let's meet at the Red Rooster House. It's been a while since I've been there.

Corinna: Good idea again. I heard they just came out with a new pasta. It should be good because Red Rooster House always has the best Italian food in town.

Sarah: When should we meet?

Lisa: Well, the movie is showing at 1:00PM, 2:00PM, 4:00PM and 6:00PM.

Corinna: Why don't we go to the 4:00PM show? We can meet at Red Rooster House at 1PM. That will give us enough time.

36. Winter Ferien – Winter Break

Tom: Hey Johann, wenn du fertig bist, dann werfe deine Sachen einfach in den Kofferraum und setzt dich in den Vordersitz.

Johann: In Ordnung Tom. Danke dass du mich nach Hause fährst. Normalerweise holen mich meine Eltern ab aber die müssen heute beide spät arbeiten.

Tom: Kein Problem, ich freue mich wenn ich helfen kann.

Johann: Übrigens, wann ist denn dein nächstes Basketballspiel?

Tom: Es ist irgendwann nach den Winter Ferien aber auf jeden Fall weit in der Zukunft. Hast du irgendwelche Pläne für die Winter Ferien?

Johann: Nein, nicht wirklich. Ich werde ins Basketballtraining gehen und arbeiten.

Tom: Arbeiten? Hast du einen neuen Job oder arbeitest du immer noch bei Twisters?

Johann: Also, Twisters war ein toller erster Job und die Leute mit denen ich gearbeitet habe waren alle nett. Aber der Schichtplan war sehr anspruchsvoll und es war schwer Schule und Arbeit unter einen Hut zu bringen.

Tom: Was machst du bei deinem neuen Job?

Johann: Ich arbeite im Bereich Technologie Verkauf. Es ist in einem Telefonzentrum. Zuerst war es ein bisschen schwierig aber jetzt habe ich mich daran gewöhnt mit Fremden am Telefon zu sprechen.

Tom: Oh, das klingt großartig.Wann hast du dort angefangen?

Johann: Ich bin bei Techmerica seit dem 1. Oktober. Hast du irgendwelche Pläne für die Ferien?

Tom: Ich plane einen Snowboard Ausflug in die Aspen. Wenn du nicht zu beschäftigt in der Arbeit bist, solltest du mitkommen.

Johann: Oh, das klingt nach Spaß! Danke für die Einladung.

WINTER BREAK

Tom: Hey Johann, if you're ready to go just throw all of your stuff in the trunk and ride in the front seat.

Johann: Alright, Tom. Thank you for giving me a ride home. Usually my parents pick me up, but they had to work late tonight.

Tom: No worries, I'm glad I could help.

Johann: By the way, when is our next basketball game?

Tom: It is sometime after winter break, but anyways it's a long time from now. Have you made any plans for the break though?

Johann: Not really. Other than going to basketball practice, I'll just be working.

Tom: Working? Did you get a new job or are you still working at Twisters?

Johann: Well, Twisters was a good first job and the people were really great to work with. However, the schedule was very demanding which made it difficult to go to school and work.

Tom: Well, what are you doing now at your new job?

Johann: I am working in technology sales. It's at a call center. It was a little difficult at first, but now I am used to talking to strangers on the phone.

Tom: Oh, that sounds great. When did you start the new job?

Johann: I have been with Techmerica since October 1st. Do you have any plans for break?

Tom: I am planning a snowboarding trip to Aspen. You should come if you're not too busy at the new job.

Johann: Oh, that sounds like fun! Thank you for the invitation.

37. Besuch beim Arzt – Visiting The Doctor

Arzt: Guten morgen Anna.

Anna: Guten Morgen, Doktor.

Arzt: Ich sehe in deinen Unterlagen, dass du seit einem Monat sehr müde bist und dann auch Migräne bekommen hast.

Hattest du auch Magenprobleme und Fieber?

Anna: Nein, Doktor.

Arzt: Lass mich eine schnelle Untersuchung machen.

Arzt: Bitte atme tief ein und halte die Luft an und dann atme aus. Noch einmal bitte.

Arzt: Hast du deine Ernährung vor kurzem geändert, ich sehe du hast Veränderungen in deinem Gewicht?

Anna: Ich habe fünf Pfund abgenommen, aber ich habe meine Ernährung nicht geändert.

Arzt: Leidest du an Schlaflosigkeit?

Anna: Es ist schwer einzuschlafen wenn ich ins Bett gehe. Ich wache auch oft in der Nacht auf.

Arzt: Trinkst du Alkohol oder rauchst du Zigaretten?

Anna: Nein.

Arzt: Es sieht so aus als hättest du eine Lungenentzündung. Ich sehe außerdem keine anderen Probleme. Ruhe dich etwas aus und bewege dich ein bisschen.

Ich gebe dir ein Rezept für die Lungenentzündung. Bist du gegen irgendwelche Medikamente allergisch?

Anna: Nein, nicht dass ich wüsste.

Arzt: In Ordnung. Nehme dieses Medikament dreimal täglich nach dem Essen.

Anna: Dankeschön, Doktor.

Arzt: Bitteschön.

VISITING THE DOCTOR

Doctor: Good morning, Anna.

Anna: Good morning, doctor.

Doctor: Looking at your information, I see that you started feeling tired about a month ago, and then you started having migraines.

Have you also had an upset stomach and fever?

Anna: No, doctor.

Doctor: Let me do a quick physical checkup.

Doctor: Please take a deep breath, hold your breath, and then exhale. One more time please.

Doctor: Have you made any changes to your diet or seen any fluctuation in your weight recently?

Anna: I lost five pounds recently, but I haven't changed my diet at all.

Doctor: By chance do you suffer from insomnia?

Anna: It is difficult for me to fall asleep when I go to bed. I also wake up a lot during the night.

Doctor: Do you drink or smoke cigarettes?

Anna: No.

Doctor: It appears that you have pneumonia. Besides that, I do not see any other problems. For now, get some rest and do some exercise.

I am going to give you a prescription for the pneumonia. Are you allergic to any medications?

Anna: Not that I am aware of.

Doctor: Alright. Take this medication three times a day after you eat.

Anna: Thank you, doctor.

Doctor: You are welcome.

38. DER MARKT – THE MARKET

Laura: Lea, bevor Mama heute Morgen in die Arbeit gegangen ist, hat sie mich gebeten einkaufen zu gehen. Das Problem ist, ich muss mein Schulprojekt zu ende machen. Kannst du bitte für mich gehen?

Lea: Ich habe meine Hausarbeit erledigt also kann ich für dich einkaufen gehen. Was braucht Mama denn?

Laura: Neben Hühnchen, Fisch und Gemüse können wir kaufen was wir als Snack und zum Frühstück wollen. Sie will dass wir genug für die ganze Woche einkaufen.

Lea: Möchtest du irgendwas bestimmtes zum Frühstück?

Laura: Nur etwas Haferbrei, so wie immer.

Lea: Ich will nicht jeden Tag Haferbrei, ich kaufe ein paar Pfannkuchen und Sirup.

Laura: Wenn du sie findest, kannst du bitte die neuen Gluten freien Pfannkuchen in der Gesundheitsabteilung kaufen. Ich möchte wissen ob die anders schmecken.

Lea: Haben wir genug Kaffee und Sahne für Mama und Papa?

Laura: Ja haben wir. Kannst du auch Milch kaufen bitte, wir haben fast keine mehr.

Lea: Was möchtest du als Snack?

Laura: Chips sind in Ordnung für mich. Du willst bestimmt die Schokoladenkekse.

Lea: Ich kenne mich, ich glaube es ist besser wenn ich all die Dinge aufschreibe ansonsten vergesse ich alles bis ich im Supermarkt bin. Ich will nicht zwei mal gehen müssen!

THE MARKET

Laura: Lea, before mom left for work this morning she asked me to go grocery shopping. The problem is that I need to finish my school project. Can you go for me?

Lea: I am finished with my chores, so I can go to the store for you. What did mom want you to buy?

Laura: Besides chicken, fish and vegetables, we can buy whatever else we want for snacks and breakfast. She basically wanted me to buy enough groceries for the entire week.

Lea: Is there anything specific you want for breakfast?

Laura: I guess some oatmeal as usual.

Lea: I don't want oatmeal every day. I will buy some pancakes and syrup then.

Laura: If you can find it, get the new gluten free pancakes in the health section please. I want to see if it tastes any different.

Lea: Is there still enough coffee and cream for mom and dad?

Laura: Yes, there is. In fact, you should buy some milk also. We're almost out of it.

Lea: Next, what do you want for snacks?

Laura: Some chips would be fine with me. You probably want your chocolate cookies.

Lea: Knowing myself it's probably better that I write all these things down or else I will forget them by the time I get to the market. I would hate to have to make two trips!

39. Eine Wohnung Mieten – Let's Get An Apartment

Patrick: Hey Johann. Was machst du hier?

Johann: Ich suche nach einer Wohnung zur miete. Was machst du hier? Suchst du auch nach einer Wohnung?

Patrick: Ja. Das Haus meiner Eltern ist sehr weit weg und ich möchte eine Wohnung finden die näher an der Schule und an meiner Arbeit ist.

Johann: Ok, ja das macht Sinn. Ich habe mich immer noch nicht entschieden ob ich in dem Schlafsaal bleiben möchte oder ob ich meine eigene Wohnung nehmen soll.

Patrick: Also nach was suchst du?

Johann: Ich brauche nicht viel ehrlich gesagt. Alles was ich brauche ist etwas das groß genug für mein Bett und meinen Schreibtisch ist. Natürlich soll es auch eine Küche haben damit ich kochen kann und etwas Geld sparen kann.

Patrick: Das klingt genau nach dem was ich auch suche. Ich kann nicht Vollzeit arbeiten so wie im Sommer. Ich werde die meiste Zeit lernen und nicht so viel arbeiten können. Alles was ich brauche ist etwas sicheres, leises und sauberes.

Johann: Ein weiteres Problem ist, dass ich die Miete alleine für eine ganze Wohnung zahlen muss. Die meisten die ich bis jetzt gesehen habe waren sehr teuer.

Patrick: Hast du schon mal daran gedacht eine Wohnung zu teilen? Wenn du willst könnten wir eine zwei Zimmer Wohnung finden und zusammen wohnen. Das ist vielleicht der günstigere Weg.

Johann: Das könnte unser Problem lösen, willst du es versuchen?

Patrick: Ja, das könnte eine gute Idee sein. Lass uns diese Wohnung anschauen, mal sehen ob wir sie mögen.

Let's Get An Apartment

Patrick: Hey, Johann. What are you doing here?

Johann: I am looking for an apartment to rent. What are you doing here? Are you looking for an apartment also?

Patrick: Yes. My parents' house is really far away so I'd like to find an apartment that is closer to school and my job.

Johann: Ok, that makes sense. I still haven't decided if I want to stay in the dorms or get my own apartment.

Patrick: So, what are you looking for?

Johann: I don't need much to be honest. All I need is a place big enough for my bed and desk. Of course, it needs to have a kitchen so that I can cook my meals and save a little bit of money.

Patrick: That sounds like what I'm looking for too. I can't work full-time like I did during the summer. I will be spending most of my time studying so I won't be able to work as much. All I need is something safe, quiet and clean.

Johann: The other issue is paying for an entire apartment for myself. Most places I have seen are very expensive.

Patrick: Have you thought about sharing an apartment? If you want, we can find a two-bedroom apartment and share it. It may be cheaper that way.

Johann: That could solve our problem. Do you want to try it?

Patrick: Yes, that could be a great idea. Let's go check this one out and see if we like it.

40. Der Zeugenstand – The Concesssion Stand

Simon: Da drüben ist ein Imbiss Stand. Wollt ihr zwei irgendwas?

Daniela: Nichts für mich, Danke. Ich habe schon eine Flasche Wasser.

Karl: Ich will eine Tüte Chips und ein kaltes Bier. Bist du sicher du willst keinen Hot Dog Daniela?

Daniela: Ich bin sicher. Meine Mama kocht heute Abend ein Steak und ich will sicher gehen, dass ich hier nicht zu viel esse.

Karl: Daniela, du hast so Glück, dass deine Mama so gut kochen kann. Simon du musst unbedingt ihren Blaubeerkuchen probieren. Ehrlich, es gibt keinen besseren Kuchen in der Stadt.

Daniela: Tatsächlich backt meine Mama heute Abend ihren Blaubeerkuchen! Wenn du willst dann hebe ich dir ein Stück auf Simon.

Simon: Meinst du das ernst? Das wäre super.

Daniela: Was ist mit dir Karl? Willst du auch ein Stück Kuchen?

Simon: Karl, du solltest deinen Snack und das Bier jetzt holen wenn du es immer noch willst. Es ist fast 15 Uhr und die Vorstellung fängt bald an.

Karl: Letzte Möglichkeit etwas zu bekommen. Seid ihr sicher dass ihr nichts wollt?

Daniela: Ich bin mir sicher, Danke Karl.

Simon: Ich auch Karl.

Karl: Ok, haltet meinen Platz frei, ich bin gleich wieder da.

THE CONCESSION STAND

Simon: There is a food stand over there. Do you two want anything?

Daniela: Nothing for me, thanks. I already have my bottle of water.

Karl: I want a bag of chips and a cold beer. Are you sure you do not want a hot dog, Daniela?

Daniela: I am quite sure. My mom is cooking a good steak dinner, and I want to make sure I don't eat too much here.

Karl: Daniela, you are so lucky to have such a good cook for a mother. Simon, you have to taste her blueberry pie one of these days. Honestly, there's no better pie in this whole town.

Daniela: In fact, my mom is baking her blueberry pie tonight! If you would like, I will save you a piece, Simon.

Simon: Don't tease me with a good time! I would love that.

Daniela: How about you, Karl? A piece of cake for you too?

Simon: Karl, you better get your snacks and beer now if you still want them. It is almost 3:00PM, and the show is about to start.

Karl: Last chance to get something. Are you guys sure you don't want anything?

Daniela: I am sure, thank you Karl.

Simon: Me neither, Karl.

Karl: Ok, save my seat and I will be right back.

41. MITTAGESSEN – LUNCHTIME

Emily: Tina, kann ich bitte dein Handy ausleihen um meine Mutter nach dem Mittagessen anzurufen?

Tina: Ja natürlich Emily. Vergiss nicht ihr schöne Grüße von uns auszurichten.

Maria: Emily kannst du mir bitte den Pfeffer geben?

Emily: Sicher, hier bitteschön.

Maria: Und auch das Salz bitte. Dankeschön.

Emily: Bitteschön.

Tina: Macht es euch was aus wenn wir im Strand Buchladen vorbei schauen bevor wir ins Kino gehen?

Emily: Nein, überhaupt nicht.

Maria: Ich habe gehört die haben eine neue Buchauswahl also würde ich gerne dort hin und sehen was sie haben.

Tina: Ich habe zu viel Essen bestellt. Möchte jemand was von meinem Essen probieren?

Emily: Ja, ich würde gerne. Es sieht sehr lecker aus.

Tina: Was ist mit dir Maria?

Maria: Nein, Danke. Ich habe schon genug gegessen.

Emily: Tina, möchtest du meine Fajitas probieren?

Tina: Ja bitte.

Emily: Hier bitte. Möchtest du noch mehr?

Tina: Oh, das ist mehr als genug! Dankeschön.

Maria: Ich denke wir sind alle fertig mit dem Essen? Wir sollten jetzt los damit wir den Verkehr vermeiden können ansonsten kommen wir zu spät.

Tina: Ich bin bereit zu gehen wenn ihr es auch seid.

Emily: Ich auch. Gehen wir.

LUNCHTIME

Emily: Tina, May I borrow your cell phone to call my mother after lunch?

Tina: Yes, of course, Emily. Don't forget to tell her we said hello.

Maria: Emily, could you pass the pepper, please?

Emily: Certainly, here you are.

Maria: And the salt too, please. Thank you.

Emily: You're welcome.

Tina: Would either of you mind if we stop by Strand Bookstore on the way to the movie?

Emily: No, not at all.

Maria: I heard they have a new book selection so I would love to stop by and check it out.

Tina: I ordered too much food. Would anybody care to try some of my food?

Emily: Yes, I would like some. It looks delicious.

Tina: How about you, Maria?

Maria: No, thank you. I have enough food already.

Emily: Tina, would you like to taste one of my fajitas?

Tina: Yes, please.

Emily: Here you go. Do you want another?

Tina: Oh, that is more than enough! Thank you.

Maria: I imagine we are all finished eating? We should leave now to avoid the traffic; otherwise we will be late.

Tina: I am ready to leave whenever you all are.

Emily: So am I. Let's go.

42. Nach einem Job suchen – Searching For A Job

Mathilde: Hi Paul, es ist schön dich zu sehen.

Paul: Finde ich auch Mathilde. Es ist eine Weile her als ich dich das letzte Mal gesehen habe.

Mathilde: Ja, das letzte Mal als wir uns gesehen haben war Halloween. Wie läuft es so?

Paul: Alles ok. Es wäre besser wenn ich einen neuen Job hätte.

Mathilde: Wieso suchst du nach einem neuen Job?

Paul: Also ich habe letzte Woche meinen Abschluss gemacht. Jetzt möchte ich einen Job im Finanzmarkt.

Mathilde: Suchst du schon lange nach einem neuen Job?

Paul: Habe diese Woche erst angefangen.

Mathilde: Du hast einen Lebenslauf, ja?

Paul: Ja.

Mathilde: Dann mach dir keine Sorgen. Du hast viel Ehrgeiz und ich weiß dass du all deine Energie in das investierst das du machen willst. Außerdem ist der Arbeitsmarkt gerade sehr gut, alle Firmen brauchen Finanz Analytiker.

Paul: Ich hoffe es. Danke für deinen Ratschlag.

SEARCHING FOR A JOB

Mathilde: Hi Paul, it is good to see you.

Paul: Same here, Mathilde. It has been a long time since I last saw you.

Mathilde: Yes, the last time we saw each other was around Halloween. How is everything?

Paul: I am doing OK. It would be better if I had a new job.

Mathilde: Why are you looking for a new job?

Paul: Well, I graduated last week. Now, I want to get a job in the Finance field.

Mathilde: Have you been looking for a new job for a while?

Paul: I just started this week.

Mathilde: You have prepared a resume, right?

Paul: Yes.

Mathilde: I wouldn't worry then. You have a lot of ambition and I know you will put all of your energy into getting what you want. Besides, the job market is really good right now, and all companies need financial analysts.

Paul: I hope so. Thank you for the advice.

43. Vorstellungsgespräch – Job Interview

Hans: Willkommen Chris. Lass uns das Vorstellungsgespräch beginnen. Bist du bereit?

Chris: Ja, ich bin bereit.

Hans: Großartig. Zu aller erst möchte ich mich richtig Vorstellen. Ich bin der Logistik Manager der Firma. Ich muss so schnell wie möglich eine Einstiegspostion besetzen.

Chris: Wunderbar. Können Sie mir etwas mehr über die Position und Ihre Erwartungen erzählen?

Hans: Der neue Angestellte wird zusammen mit der Fertigungsabteilung arbeiten. Es ist außerdem eine Voraussetzung, das die Bank jeden Tag kontaktiert wird.

Chris: Welche Art von Qualifikationen brauchen Sie?

Hans: Wir brauchen jemanden mit einem 4 jährigem Universitätsabschluss in Betriebswirtschaft. Berufserfahrung wäre auch hilfreich.

Chris: Nach was für einer Art Berufserfahrung suchen Sie?

Hans: Allgemeine Büroarbeit ist in Ordnung. Wir suchen nicht nach einer Menge Erfahrung. Für die richtige Person bieten wir auch Training im Job an.

Chris: Das ist großartig!

Hans: Was sind Ihre Stärken? Wieso sollten wir Sie einstellen?

Chris: Ich bin fleißig und lerne sehr schnell. Ich bin sehr bemüht zu lernen und ich komme mit Jedem gut klar.

Hans: In Ordnung. Ihnen macht es nichts aus lange Stunden zu arbeiten oder?

Chris: Nein, das macht mir überhaupt nichts aus.

Hans: Können Sie mit Stress umgehen?

Chris: Ja. Als ich in die Schule gegangen bin, habe ich jedes Semester an 5 Kursen teilgenommen und nebenbei mindestens 25 Stunden in der Woche gearbeitet.

Hans: Haben Sie irgendwelche Fragen für mich?

Chris: Nein, ich denke ich habe Verstanden was das für ein Job ist.

Hans: Ok, Chris. Es war schön Sie kennenzulernen. Danke dass Sie gekommen sind.

Chris: Es war sehr schön Sie kennenzulernen. Dankeschön für das Vorstellungsgespräch.

Job Interview

Hans: Welcome Chris. Let's start the interview. Are you ready?

Chris: Yes, I am.

Hans: Great. First of all, let me properly introduce myself. I am the company Logistics Manager. I need to fill an entry-level position as soon as possible.

Chris: Wonderful. Could you tell me a little bit about the position and your expectations?

Hans: The new employee will have to work closely with the manufacturing department. There is also a requirement to deal with the bank on a daily basis.

Chris: What type of qualifications do you require?

Hans: I require a four-year college degree in business administration. Some previous work experience would be helpful.

Chris: What kind of experience are you looking for?

Hans: General office work is fine. I do not require a lot of experience. There will be on the job training for the right person.

Chris: That is great!

Hans: What are your strengths? Why should I hire you?

Chris: I am a hard-working person and a fast learner. I am very eager to learn, and I get along fine with everyone.

Hans: Alright. You do not mind working long hours, do you?

Chris: No, I do not mind at all.

Hans: Can you handle pressure?

Chris: Yes. When I was going to school, I took 5 courses each semester while working at least twenty-five hours every week.

Hans: Do you have any questions for me at this time?

Chris: No, I think I have a pretty good understanding of the job.

Hans: Ok, Chris it was nice meeting you. Thank you for coming.

Chris: Nice meeting you too. Thank you for seeing me.

44. Eine Präsentation halten – Giving A Presentation

Mila: Ich halte eine Präsentation über Klimawandel am Freitag und ich bin so nervös.

Olga: Es gibt viele Dinge die du tun kannst damit du nicht so aufgeregt bist sondern mehr Selbstbewusst.

Mila: Was soll ich tun Olga?

Olga: Hast du schon zum Thema recherchiert?

Mila: Ich habe schon sehr viel recherchiert und ich weiß dass ich fast jede Frage beantworten kann die mir gestellt wird.

Olga: Erstelle eine Übersicht über deine Präsentation.

Mila: Du hast Recht. Das wird mir helfen alle Informationen zu organisieren.

Olga: Ja. Es wird dir helfen was du als erstes, als zweites und als drittes nennen solltest. Gute Idee! Es ist wichtig das du Fakten hast die deine Präsentation unterstützen. Du willst ja dass deine Präsentation glaubwürdig ist.

Mila: Ich mache das sofort! Dankeschön.

Olga: Du wirst eine tolle Präsentation halten.

GIVING A PRESENTATION

Mila: I will have to give a presentation on global warming on Friday, and I am so nervous.

Olga: There are a lot of things you can do to make you feel more confident and less nervous.

Mila: What should I do, Olga?

Olga: Have you done your research on the topic?

Mila: In fact, I have done a lot of research on the subject, and I know I can answer almost any questions I will receive from the audience.

Olga: Make sure to create an outline of your presentation.

Mila: You're right. This will help me organize all of the information.

Olga: Yes. It will help you figure out what you should present first, second, third... Good idea! It is important to have facts to support your presentation. You want the presentation to be credible.

Mila: I'm going to do that right now! Thank you.

Olga: You're going to have a great presentation.

45. Studienabschluss – Graduation

Lisa: Das ist ein sehr schöner Blumenstrauß. Für wen ist der?

Anna: Die Blumen sind für meine Schwester Silvia. Sie hat heute ihre Abschlussfeier.

Lisa: Der war bestimmt sehr teuer.

Anna: Ich habe siebzig Euro bezahlt.

Lisa: Das ist ziemlich teuer.

Anna: Meine Schwester hat die letzten vier Jahre sehr hart für ihren Abschluss gearbeitet. Für mich ist es Wert so viel Geld dafür auszugeben.

Lisa: Das ist sehr nett von dir. Ich wünschte wir würden heute den Abschluss machen. Das ist so aufregend!

Anna: Wir haben nur noch drei Jahre vor uns und dann sind wir auch fertig. Das kommt schneller als wir denken. Die Zeit vergeht so schnell.

GRADUATION

Lisa: That is a wonderful bouquet of flowers. Who is it for?

Anna: These flowers are for my sister Silvia. She is graduating today.

Lisa: It must have cost you a fortune.

Anna: I paid seventy Euro for them.

Lisa: That is quite expensive.

Anna: My sister worked very hard the last four years for her degree. To me spending that amount of money on her is worth it.

Lisa: That is very nice of you. I wish we were graduating today. This is so exciting!

Anna: We only have another three years and we will be done also. We'll be graduating before we realize it. Time goes by very fast.

46. Halloween – Halloween

Elena: Kannst du glauben das morgen Halloween ist Andrea? Die Zeit vergeht so schnell. Heute ist der 30. Oktober! Hast du schon entschieden was für ein Kostüm du anziehst?

Andrea: Ich habe mich noch nicht entschieden. Ich möchte mich entweder als Toaster oder als Gangster Rapper verkelieden. Ich habe mich immer gefragt wieso es Tradition ist sich an Halloween zu verkleiden.

Elena: Verkleiden macht so viel mehr Spaß!

Andrea: Ja ich erinnere mich wie viel Spaß ich hatte als mich Mama letztes Jahr in einem Katzenkostüm mitgenommen hat. Weißt du schon als was du dich verkleiden möchtest Elena?

Elena: Ich möchte ein Streifenhörnchen sein!

Andrea: Das ist eine großartige Idee!

Elena: Großartig! Also du gehst als Gangster Rapper und ich gehe als Streifenhörnchen. Lass uns Mama fragen ob wir morgen alleine nach süßem oder saurem Fragen dürfen.

Andrea: Ok, lass uns Mama fragen!

HALLOWEEN

Elena: Can you believe that tomorrow is Halloween Andrea? Time goes by so fast! Today is October 30th! Have you already decided what costume you want to wear?

Andrea: I'm still undecided. I want to wear either a toaster costume or a gangster rapper costume. I have always wondered why it's a tradition to dress up for Halloween.

Elena: Dressing up makes celebrating the holiday much more fun!

Andrea: Yes, I remember having a lot of fun last year when mom took me around in a cat outfit. Do you know what you want to be yet, Elena?

Elena: I want to be a chipmunk!

Andrea: That's a great idea!

Elena: Great! So, you will be a gangster rapper and I will be a chipmunk. Let's go ask mom if we can go trick-or-treating tomorrow night by ourselves.

Andrea: Ok, let's go ask mom!

47. In einem Hotel – At a Hotel

Hotel Rezeptionist: Guten Abend.

Francesco: Hallo, guten Abend. Meine Frau und ich brauchen bitte ein Zimmer für die Nacht. Haben sie eins frei?

Hotel Rezeptionist: Haben sie eine Reservierung?

Francesco: Leider haben wir keine Reservierung.

Hotel Rezeptionist: Ok, ich sehe mal nach was wir haben. Es sieht aus als hätten Sie Glück. Wir haben noch ein Zimmer frei.

Francesco: Fantastisch. Wir sind den ganzen Tag gefahren und sind jetzt sehr müde. Wir brauchen nur ein Zimmer in dem wir für die restliche Nacht entspannen können.

Hotel Rezeptionist: Das Zimmer sollte in Ordnung für Sie sein. Es ist ein gemütliches Zimmer mit einem extra großen Bett und einer Küche.

Francesco: Wie viel kostet das pro Nacht?

Hotel Rezeptionist: Das Zimmer kostet €179. Ist da noch jemand im Zimmer mit Ihnen?

Francesco: Nur wir zwei. Ich weiß, dass es schon spät ist, aber ist irgendwo noch ein Restaurant das offen hat?

Hotel Rezeptionist: Das Restaurant in unserem Hotel ist noch für eine Stunde offen. Möchten Sie für das Zimmer mit einer Kredit Karte bezahlen?

Francesco: Ja. Hier bitte.

Hotel Rezeptionist: Dankeschön. Das ist alles. Ich wünsche Ihnen noch eine gute Nacht.

At a Hotel

Hotel Receptionist: Good evening.

Francesco: Hello, good evening. My wife and I need a room for the night please. By chance do you have one available?

Hotel Receptionist: Do you have a reservation?

Francesco: Unfortunately, we do not have a reservation.

Hotel Receptionist: Ok. Let me check and see what we have. It looks like you're in luck. We have only one room left.

Francesco: Excellent. We have been driving all day and we're very tired. We just need a place to relax for the rest of the night.

Hotel Receptionist: This room should do just fine then. It is a cozy room with a king size bed and full kitchen.

Francesco: How much is it for the night?

Hotel Receptionist: It's €179 for the room. Is there anyone else staying in the room with you?

Francesco: It's just the two of us. I know that it's late at night, but is there any restaurant open nearby?

Hotel Receptionist: There's a restaurant open for another hour in the hotel. Do you want to pay for the room with a credit card?

Francesco: Yes. Here you go.

Hotel Receptionist: Thank you. You're all set. Enjoy the rest of the night.

48. Ein Austauschstudent – A Foreign Exchange Student

Andreas: Hallo, sind Sie Frau Morgan?

Frau Morgan: Ja, das bin ich. Du musst Andreas sein. Wir haben dich erwartet.

Andreas: Ich sollte schon vor zwei Tagen landen aber mein Flug aus Kolumbien war verspätet.

Frau Morgan: Ich bin froh das du sicher angekommen bist, das ist am wichtigsten. Möchtest du etwas Tee?

Andreas: Ja sehr gerne, wenn es nicht zu viele Umstände macht. Sie haben ein wunderschönes Zuhause.

Frau Morgan: Dankeschön. Wir sind vor fünf Jahren von Kolumbien nach Kalifornien gezogen und haben uns entschieden dieses Haus zu kaufen. Wir lieben es sehr!

Andreas: Ich habe ein Geschenk mitgebracht.

Frau Morgan: Das wäre doch nicht nötig gewesen. Das ist eine wunderschöne Kette. Dankeschön. Wie lange bleibst du denn?

Andreas: Ich plane für fünf Monate in Kalifornien zu bleiben um mein Englisch zu verbessern. Ich bin sehr aufgeregt in die englische Schule zu gehen und zu lernen.

Frau Morgan: Ich zeige dir dein Zimmer und dann kannst du dich entspannen. Du musst sehr müde sein nach all dem Reisen.

A Foreign Exchange Student

Andreas: Hello, are you Mrs. Morgan?

Mrs. Morgan: Yes, I am. You must be Andreas. We have been expecting you.

Andreas: I was supposed to arrive two days ago, but my flight out of Colombia was delayed.

Mrs. Morgan: Well, I'm glad that you made it safely, that is what is most important. Would you like some tea?

Andreas: I would love some, if it's not too much trouble. You have a beautiful home.

Mrs. Morgan: Thank you. We moved to California from Colombia five years ago and decided to buy this house. We absolutely love it.

Andreas: I brought you a gift.

Mrs. Morgan: Oh, you shouldn't have. This is a beautiful necklace. Thank you. How long will you be here for?

Andreas: You're welcome. I plan to stay in California for five months to practice speaking English. I am really excited to go to the English school and learn.

Mrs. Morgan: Well, let me show you your room and you can relax. You must be tired from all of the traveling.

49. Aufschub – Procrastination

Stefan: Hast du deinen Forschungs Bericht schon geschrieben? Der muss in zwei Wochen fertig sein.

Melanie: Nein, ich habe noch nicht damit angefangen. Ich habe viel Zeit es nächste Woche zu machen.

Stefan: Ich kann mich genau erinnern, dass du das letzte Woche auch schon gesagt hast und auch die Woche davor. Du hast so viel Freizeit in den Ferien du solltest es jetzt machen.

Melanie: Das Problem ist, dass ich mir wirklich schwer tue in dem Kurs und ich glaube ich brauche Nachhilfe. Ansonsten falle ich vielleicht durch.

Stefan: Ich habe eine Lösung. Hör auf darüber nach zu denken dass du Hilfe brauchst und suche dir Nachhilfe.

Melanie: Du hast Recht. Ich muss produktiv sein und mir Hilfe suchen. Ich fange gleich morgen damit an.

Stefan: Morgen? Nein, du musst heute Hilfe suchen!

Melanie: Ich weiß, ich mach nur Witze. Ich mache es heute.

Procrastination

Stefan: Have you written your research report yet? It's due in two weeks.

Melanie: No, I haven't started working on it yet. I have plenty of time to do it next week though.

Stefan: I distinctly remember that's what you said last week and the week before that. Since you have so much free time during the holiday you should get it done.

Melanie: The problem is that I am struggling in that class and I think I might need to get a tutor. Otherwise I might fail the entire class.

Stefan: I have a solution. Stop thinking about getting help and get a tutor.

Melanie: You're right. I need to be proactive and get help. I'll start looking tomorrow.

Stefan: Tomorrow? No, you have to find one today!

Melanie: I know, I'm just kidding. I will do it today.

50. Wo ist mein Bruder – Where's My Brother

Leonie: Ich kann meinen kleinen Bruder Daniel nicht finden. Ich dachte er ist hinter mir aber jetzt ist er weg. Bitte helfen Sie mir.

Polizeibeamter: Er ist wahrscheinlich in der Menge verloren gegangen. Es sind eine Menge Leute unterwegs um für die Feiertage einzukaufen. Was hat er denn für Klamotten an?

Leonie: Er hat eine blaue Jacke und eine schwarze kurze Hose an. Er ist erst 5 Jahre alt.

Polizeibeamter: Ich denke ich habe gesehen wie er in die Umkleidekammer gegangen ist. Lass mich nachsehen. Hat er blonde Haare?

Leonie: Ja, haben Sie ihn gefunden?

Polizeibeamter: Nein, das war er nicht. Lass uns im Spielzeugladen neben an nachsehen.

Leonie: Er liebt es mit Lego zu spielen. Darauf hätte ich auch kommen können.

Polizeibeamter: Ich sehe viele Kinder überall. Ist eines von denen dein Bruder?

Leonie: Daniel! Da bist du, lauf nicht nochmal weg! Du hast mich zu Tode erschreckt!

Polizeibeamter: Bitte passe auf ihn auf damit das nicht noch einmal passiert. Es kann sehr gefährlich sein wenn er ganz alleine rumläuft.

Leonie: Sie haben Recht. Ich passe ab jetzt besser auf.

Polizeibeamter: In Ordnung. Jetzt geh zu deinen Eltern und einen schönen Tag noch.

Leonie: Dankeschön für Ihre Hilfe.

WHERE'S MY BROTHER

Leonie: I can't find my little brother, Daniel. I thought he was right behind me and now he's missing. Please help me.

Police officer: He probably got lost in the crowd. There are a lot of people shopping for the holidays. What kind of clothes is he wearing?

Leonie: He has a blue jacket and black shorts. He's only 5 years old.

Police officer: I think I saw him go into the dressing room. Let me check. Does he have blonde hair?

Leonie: Yes. Did you find him?

Police officer: No, that was not him. Let's check the toy store next door.

Leonie: He loves playing with Legos, I should have thought of that!

Police officer: I see a lot of children everywhere. Are any of them your brother?

Leonie: Daniel! There you are, don't you wander off like that again! You scared me to death!

Police officer: Please keep an eye on him so that this doesn't happen again. It can be dangerous wandering around all by himself.

Leonie: You're right. I will take better care of watching him.

Police officer: Alright. Now go find your parents and have a good day.

Leonie: Thank you officer for all of your help.

CONCLUSION

Well reader, we hope that you found these dual language dialogues helpful. Remember that the best way to learn this material is through repetition, memorization and conversation.

We encourage you to review the dialogues again, find a friend and practice your German by role playing. Not only will you have more fun doing it this way, but you will find that you will remember even more!

Keep in mind, that every day you practice, the closer you will get to speaking fluently.

You can expect many more books from us, so keep your eyes peeled. Thank you again for reading our book and we look forward to seeing you again.

ABOUT THE AUTHOR

Touri is an innovative language education brand that is disrupting the way we learn languages. Touri has a mission to make sure language learning is not just easier but engaging and a ton of fun.

Besides the excellent books that they create, Touri also has an active website, which offers live fun and immersive 1-on-1 online language lessons with native instructors at nearly anytime of the day.

Additionally, Touri provides the best tips to improving your memory retention, confidence while speaking and fast track your progress on your journey to fluency.

Check out https://touri.co for more information.

OTHER BOOKS BY TOURI

ITALIAN

Conversational Italian Dialogues: 50 Italian Conversations and Short Stories

PORTUGUESE

Conversational Portuguese Dialogues: 50 Portuguese Conversations and Short Stories

ONE LAST THING...

If you enjoyed this book or found it useful, we would be very grateful if you posted a short review.

Your support really does make a difference and we read all the reviews personally. Your feedback will make this book even better.

Thanks again for your support!

Printed in Great Britain
by Amazon

59148584R00088